TANDEM

Light a Last Candle

One man, one Free Man, living up there in the Ice can just about survive, that is if the Aliens or the Wardens haven't actually decided to get him. But down in the south, beyond the pinewoods and almost to the Border, you can hide among people even easier than on the Ice cap. A man wouldn't be free there – he'd have to have his tag and registration paper, live under spies and surveillance by the Wardens. But I could disappear into the sort of hell chaos it was down there, and that was the main thing.

I had to go south, you see, and fast. There were rumours that something was stirring. Someone had risen up down there: a leader – a focus for men who would fight the Aliens. And it would be a new hope if some of the Mods were willing to fight as well.

This book is sold subject to the condition that it shall not, by way of trade, be lent, re-sold, hired out or otherwise disposed of without the publisher's consent, in any form of binding or cover other than that in which it is published.

Light a Last Candle

Vincent King

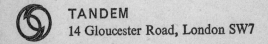

TANDEM
14 Gloucester Road, London SW7

Originally published in the United States of America by
Ballantine Books, New York
First published in Great Britain by Rapp & Whiting
Ltd, 1970

Published by Universal-Tandem Publishing Co. Ltd, 1971

Copyright © 1969 by Vincent King

Made and printed in Great Britain by
C. Nicholls & Company Ltd

CHAPTER ONE

IN the north, where the wind really *hits*, it's colder than here even. Really cold it is up there, beyond the pine fringes, north of the Tundra there's maybe fifty feet of ice, layer on layer, blizzard on blizzard, winter on long winter. Further towards the pole it must be deeper, thousands of feet of ice maybe – miles even . . . but there I suppose it's always been like that.

Every day and every day the glaciers come further, or so it seems, grinding down the hills, maybe one day there'll be nothing left. Sometimes the air smells real bad, even up there, like acid, when the wind comes from the south, from where they were changing the atmosphere.

That was why it took me so long to get out my pistol when I saw the Aliens. I mean, you don't see them too often so far north of the Borderland – in the cold – not unless they really want something. They like to be further south and warm same as everybody else.

Anyway, on the Tundra you've got to keep your weapon inside, keep it warm against your body, or the grease hardens and then it could jam. If that happened, where would you be? So maybe it takes longer to get it out – but you don't meet many people in the cold and there's usually plenty of time, you can see people coming in the snow . . . or hear them in the cold silence.

That hoverer popped up over the hill real suddenly and started trying to catch me. I hadn't heard it because the spring was coming – the sun had been warm that morning – and the end of the glacier was breaking up more than usual. Moaning it was, creaking with its stresses. When I saw the hoverer I ran away. Wouldn't you have?

I made it to some nearby ruins, got out my pistol and waited. If you can get some of the proper oil you can wear your gun outside. I've seen weapons with electrical heating too. An old man called Rutherford used to make them – he was a good gunsmith – but you can't get the cells now. When I thought about it, it was funny how he always could. A polar bear got him I heard – or maybe it was the Aliens. You didn't know what to believe – maybe he went south to that warm cave of paradise they tell children about!

So there I was, huddled up in my skins, the pistol cuddled warm into my chest to keep the bear fat warm, skulking behind a frost-splintered brick wall, waiting for what I was afraid might happen ... waiting to maybe get a shot at the Aliens – to take one with me if I was lucky.

God ... how I hate them ... how we hate them! We Free Men up north of the Borderland, I mean. They did it you know. They're the ones who tilted the planet and shifted the ice so they could get at the minerals and stuff underneath. And there was that place they made in the south; the new plants they brought; the ocean flows they changed with their alterations – the climate – so as well as shifting, the ice caps are getting bigger too. They've got whole plantations of their funny plants down south of the Border ... they say the Aliens feed them with proteins and stuff they invent. Then they make a sort of pulp they feed their Mods with, those slaves can't live on anything else now ... but that's not what those plants are really for, I bet. I'll never be a slave ... I'll die first. Then there's that great fortification they say the Aliens have built right across the world, they say there's a sort of pink paradise behind that. You don't know what to believe. I'll die before I let them get me ... I'll die, but I'll take an Alien or two with me.

Then the hoverer had me spotted. They've got some sort of thing that finds people for them when they can't see them. It's why I wear bearskins ... they can't see you white on the snow and the smell masks yours. That people-finder thing doesn't seem to work too well through pine trees either, if you can get to some. But right then they'd found me.

"OUTCAST ... BORDERMAN ... ICE LOVER ... COME OUT!" The great iron voice echoed over the valley and through the ruined buildings. A funny sound – mechanical – emphatic pauses between the words – like as if they were talking to disobedient children ... or maybe it was the search for the right sounds. I put my hand slowly into my furs and onto the butt of my pistol. The Aliens knew Free talk well enough too, because they tried that next ... it sure sounded funny in that great false voice, repeated and echoed in the ruins.

"WHY ... DO ... YOU ... WISH ... TO .. DIE ... RUNNING ... IN ... THE ... COLD?"

There wasn't anything to say, so I didn't. Pretty soon the hoverer was passing right over me. I tried to burrow into the hard snow. Then the hoverer came back and passed again so I knew they'd found me. It came back a little and stopped right over me. The warm gases and radiations were melting the snow on top of my wall, my furs were parting and starting to smell hot. I kept my face down and lay there pretending to be paralysed with fear. When they thought they saw how it was they moved the machine back a bit and settled in a clear space over there – a street it was. I was out of their sight so I got my pistol out and pulled off the safety catch.

When Aliens know where you are there's no point in running – you can't possibly get away – you've just got to stay there and do what you can for your pride's sake. You might even get lucky ... they might even go away for no reason, Aliens are like that – capricious.

The Alien came over a building a little to the right of where I'd expected. He was high – about twelve feet above the sagging roof ... drifting through the air the way they do. The blank blue spherical helmet quested about after me – maybe he'd lost his bearings crossing the buildings. All over his front there were little lights flashing. I aimed very carefully and started firing.

There's nothing like a mark seventeen. Real punch. Mine has plenty of twist left so it's pretty accurate and what you hit stays hit.

7

I fired three times, the Alien bucked in the first impact and then stabilized. The next two shots hit the bland suit hide within two inches of the first and the last one got through.

The Alien soared twenty or thirty feet into the air then crashed down onto the roof. The old beams bent, then broke and the thing crashed through in a shower of tiles, snow and rotten plastic. There was a dull thud amongst the rattle then silence.

I told you my pistol was good. Shoot through a wall! They're not so invulnerable as people say, those Aliens ... *I know*! But I never killed one easier than that ... you've just got to keep on hitting them in the same place.

That Old Rutherford I was telling you about – he gave me my pistol. He found a whole hoard of them in an old firing range when he was looking for something else. An experimental batch they were, still in their crates. He gave me two – one was really for spares, but I kept it loaded in my pack.

Somewhere I heard the hoverer start to rise. I went quickly across the icy garden ruin and kicked in the door of the house where the Alien had fallen.

There were some old ashes in the passage and some dog bones where men had been a long time ago when there were more of us. Most of what would burn had been torn down. The house was a sort of skeleton inside. The floor was scattered with fallen plastic and I pushed through sagging, hanging strands of the same stuff. The walls were cracked too ... in one place there was some wall pattern left, the colour had changed and washed out where the leaks were. I shinned up what was left of the stairs to the second floor where the Alien had lodged.

He ... you think of them as "him" ... it seems that sometimes they were human ... humanoid ... almost human – there are all sorts of stories about *that* – lay spread on the joists. He was about a foot taller than me ... his suit seemed to have held him together but something had split and some liquid eased sluggishly through to the floors below. You could hear it dripping and dripping right through to the basement.

A shadow crossed the shattered hole in the roof. I looked up and saw the hoverer maybe a hundred feet up, quartering the ruins for me. When the Alien saw where his buddy had fallen, the hoverer stopped and stood still up there. That's why they call them hoverers.

Then he decided I'd run for it and it was safe to come down and get his friend. The machine came down real close to the roof. The port dropped open and the Alien's round blue head peered down into the building.

I shrank into the shadows. I had my pistol out and aimed, but I couldn't get a clear shot through the beams and hanging stuff up there. It's no good to fire at an Alien unless you're sure of a good hit. They can blanket a whole area with sure death if they want to. That's one reason I'd come in close to the one I'd got, so the other one couldn't burn up the place the way they do ... even if he knew his buddy was dead he wouldn't do that.

The hoverer hummed louder and moved away then. It seemed like there was about four hours' silence – then I heard something scrape on the roof. The remaining Alien appeared up there, he waited a second then eased himself through the hole.

Just inside he floated still and looked about him very carefully. I know they see very well in the dark, they've got special aids for it, but maybe it wasn't dark enough in there to turn that on ... anyway, he didn't see me. He dropped down and in. He put out a sucker thing to the wall and started to examine his friend.

I saw delicate feelers spring out and probe into the mess my bullets had made. Then the Alien turned the carcass over and started to scan the dials and lights there. Then he took like a thin white cord, turned the other over, and attached it to something on the back part. He released his sucker and moved slowly back and up. I had a clear shot then.

I fired two or three times. Then the stair I was on gave way. I went crashing downstairs.

My furs protected me and I didn't stop rolling when I struck the first landing. I don't know what that last bullet hit but it sure burned!

There was like a semi explosion. A whoomp of flame and the whole top floor was a swirling lake of fire. My furs were well alight so I dived out the window. Maybe I screamed a little – or perhaps it was the Alien, someone did. I landed in a deep snowdrift. It put out my furs and near to smothered me.

There was a succession of explosions. Ordnance I guess. The fire was fiercer than ever. The flame and blast licked over the top of my drift. I was about ten feet down on the other side of the house from the door, there was an old underpass or something there, except for the ice water down my back it wasn't too bad.

It was dark in front of me – that was where the way through used to be. I went down there a bit when I'd found my pistol and came across a couple of lights burning still. They can last forever, those lights, men were good at things like that once. A few yards in the roof had come down and there was no way on so I had to go back.

After a struggle I got myself out and scuttled away just about the time what was left of the house roof fell in. Flame and smoke puffed out of the doors and windows like dragon's breath. I wondered what the Aliens carried to burn like that. Anyway, that was two less and I had to get gone before more came looking for them. That pistol was like ice on my chest but I had to put it there to warm up.

A block away I found that hoverer humming quietly to itself a few feet above the rock-hard ice on the pavement. I went over – very cautiously – the pistol ready. There were usually only two Aliens in those things, but how could you ever know?

When I got there I reckoned I had maybe twenty minutes before I needed to move – to allow a couple of hours to get clear – so I cocked up my leg and climbed in. You never know what you might find in a hoverer. Alien weapons maybe – blast tubes – you know – useful things ... maybe find an indication of where they came from and what they wanted.

I started to rummage around then I wondered why I didn't try to use the thing to get away in. At first I thought I was crazy but then I thought how I'd watched once up on the glaciers when one of those hoverers went by right under my nose and I saw right down into it. They must have thought I was a polar bear in my skins because they were real close and didn't try for me.

Anyway, there's just one big knob to control those things. Push it forward and you go forward, left to go that way and so on. Push the button on top and you go faster, take your thumb off and you stop. You control the height with a lever by the side. That's how you drive a hoverer if you ever have to. So I figured I knew enough to chance it. What did I have to lose?

I had to go south you see. I had to go south and fast. Beyond the pinewoods and to the people there, almost to the Border. You can hide in people even easier than on the ice cap. The Aliens would sure be after me – they'd have everything out to get me. Sometimes they made examples of people who fought back – had to, I suppose. I would too – if I was them.

One man, one Free Man, living up there in the ice can just about do it – survive, that is – if the Aliens or the Wardens haven't actually decided to get him. It was even possible I might have been able to stay and get away with it – but I knew I'd be safer south amongst the people. A man wouldn't be free there – he'd have to have his tag and registration paper – live under spies and surveillance by the Wardens ... travel permits and all that. But if I kept my nose clean I could disappear into the sort of hell chaos it was down there and that was the main thing.

Mind, I'd wanted to go south for a long time. There were rumours that something was stirring. Someone had risen up down there – a leader – a focus for men who would fight the Aliens. Maybe we'd really be able to do something at last. Then there were all those fables we've all heard, all those things they tell you when you're a

11

child. Anyway, I sure couldn't stay in the north, in a sort of way those Aliens just pushed me into something I'd already made up my mind to do.

So I decided to take the machine and make it south. Lose it in the woods someplace – by the time the Aliens found out what had happened I'd be long gone. If it crashed and I was killed, well then that was that and nothing would worry me any more.

The hoverer was harder than I thought. I pulled up the lift lever, we shot up about a thousand feet, and I felt sick. I let the lever go and we came down like a stone. The machine stopped short about twenty feet up and nearly broke my back. There must have been some sort of automatic control because when I got the thing going forward it steered us out of the city, all through the crumbling ruined streets, the sagging steel arch of some old bridge there ... all the other stuff left over from the Defeat. In the end I found how the "go" button locked down and relaxed. The machine took me south in ease and comfort, it was real sweet.

There are a lot of ruins, one way and another. I mean, you can't have a country like New England was and not have something left. You could see twisted girders there, all gobbed and melted in places ... the street plan of some burned and flattened city, great places down there, like sores ... all glinting with bubbled and broken glass. An alarm sounded as we went over one place like that and the hoverer took itself up a couple of hundred feet. I guess it was just playing safe – I don't think there's anything radiating dangerously down there now ... or maybe it smelled one of the plague spots ... there's danger forever from them if the bodies weren't burned.

Later on the hoverer started talking to me so I pulled out some circuit stems and it stopped. Maybe that would tell the Aliens they had a hoverer in trouble so then I knew that I had better start walking soon. A couple of miles west, a dark reef of forest scrub reached out for me so I turned the machine towards it. Small stuff it was, growing in a sheltered valley that reached up into that scoured plateau I was crossing.

About five minutes down the valley, above the first of the really tall pines I unlocked the "go" button and pushed the lever down until we landed. The machine let us down lightly in the underbrush. Then something shifted and it canted to one side. I climbed out and looked for something to burn.

After a while I got the cowl off the back and there was a drum thing connected up to what I took to be the drive unit of the antigrav. It was like the fuel cells on Rutherford's guns, but bigger. I got my knife out and stabbed holes in it, made of some sort of plastic stuff it was, it cut real easy. Thick stuff started to pour out and as it did the tank got smaller, like a balloon when you puncture it, but slower.

I went a little way down the valley and struck sparks until I had a small fire under the pines. There wasn't much snow there and the needles soon caught. When I saw the flames would reach the hoverer I moved off and started making distance.

I'd got about a mile when the machine went up. It was nearly dark by then and the fireball which climbed up over the pines was a beauty. There was a great pile of black smoke climbing up against the sky when I looked again.

The fire was pretty obvious so for safety I climbed the valley side and went about three miles south-east over the plateau into the next one. When my eyes got used to the darkness under the trees I got along quite fast. It was rough going though. Once in a while I'd cross a path but none of them were very marked. I guess they were game tracks and I kept clear of them all the same, I didn't want to meet anyone at a time like that. In those thick trees the Aliens wouldn't find me, if I avoided open spaces their detectors couldn't reach me – so I sure didn't want to risk some chance-met hunter giving me away.

I kept going all night and by dawn I was well into the thicker woods. I began to figure I might have a good chance after all.

CHAPTER TWO

IN the morning there was a still, fat smoke pall hanging above the woods a few miles behind me. Seemed like I'd burned a lot of woodland too when I fired that hoverer.

Mind, there were plenty of other hoverers about. There must have been half a dozen of them buzzing about back there like silver flies against the black smoke and the misty grey-green of the pines. The woods were pretty well alight there, but there was a breeze from the south and that kept the fire from spreading out of the valley.

The Aliens would have been there most of the night – as I said darkness doesn't seem to affect them too much. After a while the hoverers stopped circling and spread out, fanning away to the north mostly – I guess they would have expected me to run that way. They couldn't have found those dead Aliens yet. One hoverer went south with the sagging hulk of the burned one swinging beneath it. It left a faint trail of smoke against the clear sky . . . it sure was a mess. I sure got that one!

I opened one of the old tins from my pack – there are massive caches of them in the ice, they keep forever there – and ate it quick. I hoped for meat but it was peaches . . . you've got to take a chance in life. Then I headed south again, it still wasn't any time to hang about.

Pretty soon the trees were really thick and I could relax. That south wind that kept the fire in the valley brought snow first then rain. Summer was coming, it was downhill all the way and it was getting warmer all the time. I hurried on in the downpour. I didn't go right down off the hills, there was plenty of cover below but it would be sodden down there, hard going . . . and I knew there might be flies.

I hate flies. I can't stand them. They're my horror ...
everybody's got one ... the way they buzz all the time.
Flies are everything a man shouldn't be. Dishonourable
.... carrion living ... feeding on other creature's leavings – like the Mods, the once-men who live subject to
the Aliens. How can humanity ever deserve justice while
they crawl like flies? They were men once, those Mods
... that's what happens when you live on leavings, like
flies!

Old Rutherford reckoned it was maybe why I lived
up north on the Tundra – to get away from most of the
flies. "That's the *real* reason," he used to say. "You
don't always know your real reasons ..." Subconscious
– that was his word for it.

About breakfast time the third day I smelled wood-
smoke. I went forward more cautiously. You've got to
be careful about meeting people. It was still raining and
as I went forward the smoke was hanging and trapped
amongst the wet trees. I was pretty hot in my furs and
they were getting very heavy with the rain. I was thinking about maybe taking some off for a while when there
was a voice behind me.

"Who are you, mister?" Then more quickly: "I've got
a shotgun – don't turn round!" It was a woman's voice.
I froze.

"I'm just a traveller," I said. "I don't mean any
harm."

"You haven't got that chance ... you behave and I
won't shoot." She thought for a bit, then went on: "I'll
take you to my man ... you walk on through them
pines. You behave!"

I walked on the way she said. About a hundred yards
through the trees there was this clearing with a hut and
a guy was there splitting tree trunks with a sledgehammer and wedges.

On the right were two or three big piles of earth ...
round they were – conical – and smoking at the top.
Charcoal ... the man was a charcoal burner. I didn't
know you could make good charcoal with pine trees ...
still, I don't suppose it matters too much.

They were Mods of course. Most people are. The guy had the darkness of one for a start. Those great big violet infra-red eyes and the directional ears. God knows what else – inside I mean – he might be a coal eater or anything ... you can't tell what modifications there are inside. He had what was left of a carapace instead of hair, most of it had been cut away in front to widen his vision. Sometimes a carapace will just keep on growing and growing and a Mod'll have to pare it away like toenails ... just to keep on breathing.

When I got a look at the woman I saw she had the Breeder modifications. Mind, you could tell she'd been born free – second or third generation, I'd guess – but the modifications were pretty noticeable ... not that they were pretty. That great belly with two wombs, the four breasts ... the massive, open pelvis. There were traces of other modifications about her too. Her ears for example – Breeders shouldn't have directional ears like that. She said later that it'd been her grandmother who had escaped – that her mother had been born free. The modifications don't always get less though ... it took God knows how many millions of years to evolve Free Man in the first place ... that's the tragedy. Then the Aliens did what they did to us and maybe it'll never disappear ... it may not even get less ... or take millions upon millions of years to evolve out.

What's happened is that when people escape from the Aliens they breed and the modifications have got mixed into a ragbag collection of monstrosities ... bizarre ... Old Rutherford said it was. Hellish I call it ... somehow sickening and dishonourable that humans should be perverted like that. There were the bombs too ... the radiation from them didn't help either.

It'd never go ... never change ... not unless we get to know as much as the Aliens and do something about it ... I couldn't see much chance of that. It was up to us Free Men to keep ourselves pure, keep our really human genes in existence.

Some Mods hated us Free Men. They couldn't help it, some of them even tried not to show it. You can

16

understand it in a way. I knew a Free Man once who felt like Mods the way I feel about flies. It's not all one-sided. I guess the only thing that kept us from hunting and killing each other was the overall menace of the Aliens. Anyway, I kept my furs on so they wouldn't know I was a Free Man, it pays to keep quiet about that if you can.

When I came into the clearing the man turned quickly and came up with a rifle. He had old tarpaulins spread over the place, patched and drooping things on branches and poles – like a big tent – and tarred. To keep the daylight out – I guess he saw by the infra-red from the charcoal piles. It was natural for him in the darkness ... even under the trees daylight would have hurt him.

"You're an Ice Lover," he said. "What are you come here for? What do you want with us?"

"I'm going down south. Making for the people north of the Borderland. I've been lonely ... Ice Lovers get lonely. I don't want anything from you ... maybe a meal and a warm by your fire ..."

He nodded. Well – they wouldn't have anything that'd tempt anyone to steal it – maybe get shot for. He could afford to believe me. He was just being careful, you can't blame a guy for that.

"You armed – got a gun?"

"Sure." I mean – what did he expect? One thing the Aliens never bred Mods for was brains.

He grunted then stepped to one side, motioned me under the tarpaulins, towards the hut they had there. He could trust me even more then. It was as black as pitch except for a charcoal brazier in front of the hut. To him it would have been as bright as day.

"You keep your gun to yourself," he said. "You won't need it here."

After a while the Woman lit a candle and put it by me. The man I couldn't see at all. He stayed away and asked questions about the Tundra and what it was like up there. The Woman brought me bread and boiled bacon and when I had eaten I told him most of what he

17

wanted to know. Not everything. I was pretty vague about how many men there were up there, or how well armed they were. I didn't mention Free Men at all – I let on I hadn't seen any for years – which was true, by the way. As a matter of fact it meant I hadn't seen many people at all – not many Mods get up on the ice, the snow is too bright for them. I certainly didn't say anything about killing those Aliens or that I had anything to do with burning any hoverers.

The Charcoal Burner said there'd been a lot of activity up north. Hoverers going and coming, the smoke and so on . . . what he called a "great light" – by which he meant the fire. The Woman had seen the burned hoverer being carried south. I still kept quiet – you never know who might have connections active – be spies – lookers for the Aliens . . . either for gold or whether they liked it or not. Even though that guy had destroyed most of his carapace you couldn't be sure, some of them don't even know they're slaves.

After a while he revealed what he was really doing in the woods. He brought over a bottle and a couple of beakers and poured us a drink. He said it was good grain stuff, but I guess it was mostly pine knots. It was raw – but like most things, a little won't hurt you. He probably drank it all the time himself . . . not such a slow poison either. Really it was only fit to run engines on – not that it would do them much good either. In a sort of way I suppose it was a service he did. Some Mods don't care if they die or how . . . he sold them oblivion – an escape from it all. Maybe he had some special stuff for himself, I hoped he used it for guests too. Anyway, the Woman brought some dirty-looking sugar – we took a mouthful and drank the booze through that. It made it a little better.

As we got on with the drinking the Mod's tongue got looser. The Woman didn't say much. She just looked at me – stared – like she was fascinated. They wouldn't have seen too many people out that way. Dull for her. I wondered why there weren't any kids about, but her being a Breeder didn't mean too much – she was third

18

generation remember – things don't always work out exactly how the Aliens intended after the first generation. They're not omniscient – she might even be sterile, I thought. But she sure kept staring at me.

"They haven't pulled anything that far north before," said the guy. "They must be getting stronger, or braver. It can't go on – the Aliens are bound to get them. You can't do anything against the Aliens – not for long. You can't hurt 'em . . . they'll have it their way in the end."

I didn't say anything, it was a time for listening. He made to give me more booze but I stopped him. I wanted to hear everything, find out who "they" were that had pulled something in the north, I didn't want too much poison. There was a few seconds' silence while he was drinking again.

"What do you mean 'they'?" I asked, then buried my nose in my beaker to hide my interest. I saw the Woman start and begin to look worried, then she smiled in a stupid sort of way and lowered her eyes to the blue flickering charcoal. The man hesitated, then he finally spoke out of the dark.

"You ain't heard? You ain't heard word of the Riders?"

"I've been up north – couple or three years. Scavenging – I told you. I haven't heard of *nothing!*"

"Yeah . . . well . . . you seem like a straight guy . . . But it isn't good to even think about *them!* If you even mention them and the Aliens hear about it you get a Warden come knocking at your door . . . You forget it, Ice Lover! It don't do to know too much. I'm not saying any more!" He drank again, deeply.

"I can keep my trap shut."

"Yeah . . . I noticed. You don't say much. S'pose I can trust you . . . you ought to be warned . . . you seem like a good guy." He was pretty drunk by then and loved everybody. I offered him tobacco and that pleased him. He filled his old pipe and I rolled up a fag, then he went on talking. "Them . . . some men have got together and started planning to shoot Aliens. Damn foolishness. I heard they actually killed some Wardens. Ain't heard

19

they hurt any Aliens. Don't reckon you can, myself. Only bring trouble though – trying to.

"Those Riders ... they've killed a lot of spies though ... and Wardens." The Mod sat quiet for a moment, he was pretty drunk. I saw his pipe glow in the dark ... those great eyes lit suddenly as he sucked. "Course ... there was that hoverer ... two – three days back ... that one got burned up ... maybe the Underground did that. Killed themselves an Alien or two maybe ... You sure you didn't see anything?"

"I came down east of that ... maybe I saw some smoke. ..." The Mod didn't trust me. He wasn't sure – suspicious again. You couldn't blame him. "Sorry about the 'bacco – it's been frozen a long time. ..." I waited, lit my fag again. Then I tried once more. "But what about those guys ... those Riders? Bandits are they? Or mad ...? Or what ...? Hey ...! Could they be Free Men? Are there any of *them* left?"

The Mod was very still. Then he spat in the fire.

"They must be mad," I said. "I mean, taking on the Aliens ... life ain't that bad – is it? I mean ... we're living ..."

"Call it that?" He spat in the brazier again. I heard him pouring more drinks. The Woman was uneasy again. "I don't figure so much it's wrong or mad to fight the Aliens as stupid. Like I say, I'm not so sure you can hurt them. These Underground Riders – they should hide up ... keep human ideals alive – bide their time!" It was pretty funny to hear a Mod talking about *"human"* values. Still, I suppose we're mostly the same now – they've got as much right as almost any. "I don't mean they won't get anywhere," he went on. "They may have some success ... it's well worth doing ..."

"How many are there?"

"You interested?" He looked up quicky. "You don't want to get too interested unless you really mean it."

"How can I meet these guys?"

"In their Enclosure ... at the Underground ... they've got a fortification. ... Forget what I told you – forget I told you!"

20

It was all he'd say then. But it was some sort of hope. The Aliens had been on earth a long time now. Sure, there'd been some serious resistance to start with ... we had armies and even small spaceships ... rockets and bombs ... but this was the first *rising* – from inside I mean ... from under the heels of the Aliens.

After the Defeat, after the modifications and all, there hadn't been much chance of anything. It was all dim in history now – the Defeat was long ago ... it was remote in time when man last stood upright. Except for the few I mean – up on the Tundra ... out in the cold ... guys like me who'll bend for no one, especially a dirty Alien. It was a new hope if some of the Mods were willing to fight as well.

I asked the Mod again where I could meet these Underground Riders. He was sure drunk by then, just mumbled something more about the south and contacts there. I guessed he really didn't know anything – he'd just been making talk – gaining a little significance for himself by holding my interest.

Later the Woman showed me where I could lie warm near one of the charcoal piles. I put down my pack and curled up to sleep not far from where she said with my pistol under my cheek. That way no one can steal your gun and you're still armed and alive in the morning.

About two hours later I woke with a poison headache from the liquor we'd had. Then I saw the Woman coming across the clearing. She'd trodden on something and that had woken me.

In the wisps of smoke and mist, in that pale starlight she looked beautiful ... you got to remember I hadn't seen a woman for more than three years.

I knew what she wanted as soon as I saw her. The Breeders have this terrific drive that hits them at night. You couldn't call it to "make love" ... there's no love in it. It might seem the same – in the end I mean – but it isn't. It's an obsession with them ... an evil. It's just another of the things the Aliens have done to them ... to us. It's no good to get mad about it ... it's the reason

21

they're called Breeders. If they're not pregnant they can't rest until they are.

Anyway, she came for me in the night. Sobbing and sighing and reaching out for me. There was a sort of hate too in her eyes ... that's the really diabolical thing – they don't enjoy it. It wasn't her ... it was the Aliens reaching out across all her life ... it was the Aliens wanted me.

She struggled and whimpered as I held her off. I counted to ten and pushed her away. She let down her skirt and started crying.

"You too?" she asked after a bit, through her tears. I looked beyond her and saw the man in the door of his hut, against the fire in there, watching us.

I understood how it was then. That guy – her man – he wasn't a Breeder male – didn't have the modification. Poor Woman ... she had a rotten life ... she'd die mad. Breeders shouldn't fight it, no one's strong enough. Perhaps that was why she lived out here in torture – to keep away from it ... away from men and what the Aliens wanted her to be. Maybe that was why she'd chosen the Charcoal Burner to be her man. It must have been hell for her.

I up and left. She cursed me and thanked me.

I called back from the edge of the glade that I didn't have the modification either. Which is true, of course, I'm a Free Man ... free of any modifications at all. She nodded and got up to walk back to the hut. There were tears on her cheeks, you could see them wet in the firelight. You'd cry too, if you were like that. Maybe what I said made her feel better.

When she reached the door the Charcoal Burner put his arm round her shoulder and led her in. I heard him speaking softly to her.

You don't have to take part, you see. Even if you have to live in a world like ours, live in filth and oppression ... in sickness and decay ... well – you've got to live with it – but even if you don't actually *fight* you don't have to take part.

Then the man came to the door again and called after me.

"Ice Lover . . . If you want those Riders ask for Crag-head. Be careful, Ice Lover . . .!"

I went south, through the woods.

CHAPTER THREE

I KEPT right on walking all through dawn and long after the next morning. Partly I wanted to get as far south and into the people as I could, to get away quick from where I'd killed those Aliens ... away from that Charcoal Burner too, just in case. All I wanted was to sink into the people – to disappear without trace there.

Also I was excited. This was great news about the Underground Riders. This discovery of an organized rising ... the *hope* there was in it. The possibility that man would fight now ... or that some of them would ... and maybe – sometime – get back up. Maybe Mods were ready to fight at last ... maybe some were honourable after all ... more man-blood in them than I'd thought, perhaps.

I could hardly keep my hands still. All the vistas were opened right up – God knew where it might lead to.... If Craghead wasn't just a rumour that is ... and the Aliens weren't too strong.

For a while there I was singing and almost dancing as I marched and crashed through the bushes. Man – I just didn't care! I was drunk ... riding high on the possibility of hope. Underground Riders – they were really something to look forward to!

Craghead ...! I kept thinking about Craghead ... the sort of man he might be. What a *power* there was in that name! What an uplifting toughness ... the individuality it spoke of! The honesty ... the straightforward quality there ... rugged and truthful like a mountain peak! *Craghead!* what a name! It was like a song! A paean of human values!

Like Robin Hood maybe – a great hero figure – like those we half remember in history – King Arthur ...

Joan of Arc ... Pizarro – perhaps a Castro or a Kennedy! A Christ figure to spread his arms and lift us from our misery ... to save us from ourselves and the Aliens. Hope it was – *hope!*

I was too cheerful for my own good. Right then somebody up the hill tried to shoot me in the back. Maybe he was miserable and he figured I was too happy.

The heavy bullets slashed through the rain and into the pine tree in front of me. A couple of cones came down, raw, broken branches and needles. One bullet struck a stone at my feet – I felt the splinters and shards of bullet sting into my shins.

I guess I sobered up pretty quick then. I made it in a hurry into the roots of the nearest pine. I sent a shot up where the powder smoke was hanging amongst the undergrowth.

It's the way things are – and in a way it's reasonable. You met a stranger and if you thought it might come off – maybe if his back was turned – you took a shot at him. It stops guys getting too cocky. Clears the blood – lets some of the hate out. Everybody does it. If you hit the guy then you pick up his gun and ammunition – any gold he's got. It's the way things are – another of the things the Aliens have done to us. They put a lot of sheer murderousness into the modifications ... took a lot of the humanity out. Anyway – Mods or not – there are a lot of violent people in the Borderland. Now the woods were mixed, there were a lot of birches right there, and I was beginning to get south, I could expect to meet a lot more of them.

This guy that was shooting at me didn't mean anything – it was *casual* – a casual stranger trying to kill me. It happens all the time, nothing personal in it.

I reckon my second shot got quite close to him. He yelped, then shouted down about it all being a mistake and how about a truce? He said all he wanted was out and I was shooting too good and had too much gun for him.

I was flattered I guess, so when I heard him move off up the slope away from me I let him go. There wasn't

25

a lot I could have done anyway. I went on more cautiously than before. It's just the way things are.

But maybe I got overcareful, nervous perhaps, or maybe more aware, because after that I kept thinking there was someone following me. I waited a couple of times, but I saw no one . . . the feeling persisted though – you know – like eyes in your back.

Later in the day I rested up under some willows close to a stream. The trees kept dripping but I felt safer and even risked a small fire. I opened a can of sardines – you can tell them by the shape of the can – it seemed suitable by the water. I even brewed some tea. Good stuff – in the ice the best part of three hundred years. I wondered what it was like in Ceylon right then. I often wonder about Ceylon.

A hoverer went over and burned up some woodland to the north while I was there. I guess they were killing anyone they found in the woods – maybe it was that guy that tried to shoot me. Maybe he was the one who'd been following me – if anybody had.

In the evening I came across one of the old roads. Dual highway – cracked up, covered and sprouting all over with coiling brambles. I followed it along the valley.

Ahead, down there in the misty lowland I saw the lighter ribbon of the Aliens' road and – in a clearing – a small town.

The vertical smoke from the chimneys looked so welcoming and I had a vision of a real bed, so I went on down although, really, I knew better. On the way I saw a Warden patrol heading north on the Aliens' road. They were going real fast, still after whoever it was that burned that hoverer, I guess.

The town was the usual straggle of timber and turf houses set back a little from the road. The usual dirty people – all Mods of various colours and sorts – going about whatever it was they had to do. They'd be escapers some of them, as well as the second and third generation. Some of them might be still under control. . . have their communicators still active; then again

26

some might even be spies of their own free will – for money, or as sycophants – pathetically licking up to their Alien bosses.

Aliens never bother too much about escapers – they had plenty of other slaves – especially with the Breeder pens. There were a few Wardens about. There'd be a Registrar too, somewhere. I avoided them all, moved in shadows towards the smokey red light over the inn door. Not that that would have done me any good if there were any Mods about who wanted me and had the dark vision.

The inn was full of smoke, some of it was tobacco, but mostly it came from the lamps and the fire. The low room was packed with people, men and women. Some were drunk – mostly they were miserable. It was really hot in there. Mods tend to like it hot.

You should have seen the modifications they had! All sorts and mixtures ... "bizarre" was right ...! There were a few women – all Breeders ... but women with other modifications were pretty much like men – so who knew? Or cared. There were kids too ... and they would really have made you cry....

I fought over towards the bar. I kept my skins on with the collars well up so nobody would see I was a Free Man. Except for some of the Breeders who were in heat they just ignored me. I asked the landlord about a bed for the night. He looked me up and down, then said to wait.

The door opened again then the lights flickered as the Charcoal Burner came in. I think he recognized me, it would have been like daylight in there for him ... he must have seen me. I turned away quick but I thought I saw two women come in behind him. He didn't make any sign – and I didn't want him to. Life's dangerous enough without friends. Later I saw him bringing in plastic bottles of the booze he made.

Soon after that there was a scream of alarms coming down the highway. Everybody stopped talking to listen, then, when the road trucks halted outside, there was a movement towards the back of the room.

27

Seconds after the door crashed open and half a dozen Wardens burst in.

I'd found a curtained door in the gloom at the back – but I didn't have time to do anything about it. Everybody froze and looked at the Aliens' men. It was no good, the place would be surrounded by then ... one thing, those Wardens, especially when they're controlled, they're pretty efficient. Like I say, we only had time to stand and look at them.

They wanted looking at too. First there were those deadly two-foot hell tubes that were the Aliens' tamer weapons ... the ones they issued. Then there were those thick arms – with the two-inch skins – clothed in that armoured thin stuff which was so beautiful and so tough. They hardly needed that though, that thick skin the Aliens had given them would practically stop most bullets just by itself.

But what *really* stopped you were the carapaces. Thick horny things – they say the Aliens grew them, based them, on hair ... originally. Not that it was much like that now. It sprouted from the nape of the neck, started just above those grossly thickened shoulder blades, enveloped the whole face and head – just an oval opening in the front for the features. Then embedded in the semitransparency was the communicator cell. They say there's a two-inch skull under that lot, Wardens don't need too much brain with a direct communicator.

That communicator – the control thing – that was part of the brain. The Aliens had wanted real close control of the men they'd armed, so they'd had to do something special with the military modifications. A receiver and communicator – a controlling unit built up from part of the medulla was what they used. The Officer had an eye too, a biological one extra, set in his carapace. It could move independent of the others, it was for the Aliens. Right then it was focused straight ahead – the Aliens themselves weren't interested – not for the moment. Some people reckon there's an actual bit of Alien brain tissue like grafted into those control things, it

28

didn't seem likely to me ... you can't graft entirely different species – any gardener'll tell you that. There were a couple of Registrars with the Wardens.

"Papers!" grated the Registrars.

"Let's have them – your credentials ... your discs!" said the Warden Officer. They stationed themselves along the walls and pointed their weapons at us.

There was a sullen sort of movement amongst the crowd as we fished amongst our clothes. Some looked resentful – but we all accepted it.

I didn't have any papers – or a disc. I eased a hand onto my pistol instead. I'd often wondered what it'd do to one of those carapaces at close range. It looked as though I might find out if I was quick and lucky. I put my other hand round one of the oil lamps on the bar. I began to slip as quietly as I could through the press towards that curtained door I had spotted.

The Wardens began to pass through the crowd. They began to glance at discs and papers. I wasn't convinced any of them could read though.

Then – suddenly – there was an explosion of action across the room. One big guy with a beard and the dragging modification pulled out a sawed-off shotgun and gave one of the Registrars a barrel in the stomach. He got off a blast at one of the Wardens too.

I saw then how a shotgun won't touch a carapace. The blast roughened it some and knocked the Warden down but he got up right after. I guess that big guy didn't have any papers either.

The whole room stood still for a moment. I saw gunsmoke begin to curl and the Warden start to get up again. The Registrar started moaning. The people began to scatter, some of them not quickly enough.

That big guy was quick though. He'd almost got his gun loaded again before they cut him to smoking mincemeat ... those little secondary hands moved like lightning.

All the Wardens were looking that way right then so I lobbed the lamp over the heads in front of me into the middle of the floor and shoved hard for the curtain.

The yellow flame burst up and there were more screams. The Wardens backed to the door, their weapons ready.

I didn't make the curtain. Something soft clogged my movement, tripping and trapping me against the bar. I started to fight back then I felt something poke into my ribs. I looked down and saw a small silver pistol. I held my breath.

"Stand still!" a girl's voice hissed in my ear. "Don't run. They'll have the place surrounded. Cut you down like a dog!" I tried to twist and see who it was – but I couldn't, I sure didn't know that voice. Some papers and a tag thrust themselves into my hand. "Take these *quick!*"

I took them. You've got to trust someone sometime. I'd never have made it on the run anyway. I managed to turn and saw deep into a girl's eyes. Yellow they were – reflecting the growing fire – not night eyes. I was so close I couldn't see much more of her face. She felt like a Breeder though.

"Out! Out!" the Warden Officer was yelling. They went piling through the door. We struggled after them. They left the Registrar where he was for the fire … there was another too, a Warden that someone had knifed in the confusion. I don't know how you knife a Warden – not through that hide, but someone managed it.

It was raining again outside. They made us fall in in the yard and looked at our papers there by the light – or heat – of the burning inn. Nobody tried to put the fire out. Some things aren't too important. I got soaked.

My papers got me through OK. I was supposed to be a Day/G.P.W./2nd generation. A general-purpose worker is practically unmodified – except the belly, to take the filth the Aliens feed them … and that he'll probably have an IQ of about sixty. Even the Aliens haven't come up with anything better for G.P. work than the old human frame, so it fitted me pretty well. I mean, I could act stupid.

When they let us go I looked for the girl that had saved me. I hunted all through the dispersing crowd

30

but I couldn't see her. I guess it was partly that I wanted to thank her – but also I wanted to find out why, what the catch was. Nobody does anything for nothing. I couldn't find her though – she'd gone as quietly as she'd come.

Most of the people were standing with their mouths open watching the inn burn down. There were a couple of beatings going on where someone had spoken back to a Warden, I moved back out of the firelight and went down towards the highway.

Looking back near the inn I saw the Charcoal Burner climb into a battered old truck and start it up. His Woman was there too. It was a gasoline burner, that truck, an internal-combustion engine – you should have seen the exhaust! The Aliens seemed to let some people run them, I wondered why the Charcoal Burner was allowed to. Maybe they reckoned his hooch kept enough people quiet to make it worthwhile. Maybe he burned his booze in it. As I said, it was about all it was fit for.

Then the Wardens came past me and went down the road so I looked away. They eyed me up and down and I was glad there'd just been a check. When the Charcoal Burner passed he didn't look at me and neither did his Woman. They knew who I was OK, with his vision he couldn't have missed me. I wondered if, maybe, it was him that'd followed me up in the woods.

By the time I got to the road the Wardens were long gone and the Charcoal Burner's truck was well up the hillside on the other side of the road.

Mind, that road was a heck of a thing. Maybe a hundred yards wide running due north and south. The thing hung about twenty feet above the ground, it was made of that silvery-grey crystal stuff the Aliens used for everything they didn't grow. It was beautiful in the starlight – shining away into the distance. Magnificent – you had to admit it.

The Aliens used to use it for shifting really heavy loads and getting their Wardens about quickly – they didn't trust them with real hoverers. Except for the Wardens it didn't seem to get much use in those days, it was

31

almost as if the Aliens had tired of it and forgotten it was there.

But the marvellous thing is it was our conception – the idea and the routing was ours – man's. It's still there, our road, the original. Underneath ... cracked and crumbled ... in places blasted and fused ... broken up and down ... but still there, under that hanging Alien one. In a sort of way it's reassuring that ours is still there. In another way it isn't – it's a reminder of the way things are – our place now and our old one. It's a symbol. It made me want to cry.

After a while, when it had all gone quiet and the fire had burned out, I made my way back and found a shed. I kicked a cow out of there and bedded down in her warm straw.

CHAPTER FOUR

ONE thing I'd forgotten to do was to pick those stone bits out of my legs from when that guy nearly shot me in the woods. After a while, when I couldn't stand the stinging any more, I got up, lit a stump of candle I had and started picking them out with the small, clean blade of my pocket knife. You've got to be hygienic. There was nothing too big or too painful.

I was dusting on the antiseptic powder – I didn't know how much good it was, like everything else it was from the ice – when that cow, which had lain down outside, got up and I heard a female voice talking to it.

I rolled over and got my pistol. When the door opened I shoved it in the girl's face. She put her hands up and I made sure she wasn't armed. Then I relaxed and put my gun away. Not too far away.

She was a Mod all right. Like I thought, a Breeder. I knew what she wanted. I mean ... she was what she was ... she wasn't pregnant and it was night. I'd counted four breasts when I searched her, left-handed, for weapons. What would you have thought she wanted?

She had long pale blonde hair which she'd let down. Or maybe it was that she'd taken her hood off. She was short for a Breeder, a little shorter than me. They tend to be very long-waisted – have long bodies, to make room for the breasts, I suppose – she wasn't what you'd call slender, but she was certainly lighter about the belly and hips than most Breeders I'd seen.

In fact she was almost acceptable. Well ... I owed her something ... I'd give her what she wanted. Save her a night of that torture. I'd take part just this once.

I reached out for her but she stopped me.

"No – not that." She said. "Not that. You don't have to . . . I don't want you for that."

"You . . . you're a Breeder?" I was surprised and a bit angry. I found I wasn't all disinterested, that – just a little – I'd wanted her. This refusal was something new from a Breeder, usually you got to beat them off.

"No. I want to talk. Talk to you about Craghead. Put your clothes on and listen."

When I finished buttoning myself she came down on her knees beside me. She must have seen the surprise and distrust on my face. Well, would you trust a Breeder who wouldn't?

"There are drugs you know," she said quickly. "If you can get the drugs you don't have to . . . to be what the Aliens want."

"Who's Craghead?" The hell with her problems. For a secret leader a whole lot of people seemed to know about this Craghead. "What'd I want with him?" Now I'd started thinking again I mustn't give away too much. The girl ignored the question.

"I thought you didn't have the modification?" she was still on about the sex thing. Women are like that – all the time, one way or another, Mod or not – it's the biggest single thing in their minds. Never mind what they say – that's the way they are. I mumbled something meaningless about the third generation, then pointed out her own modifications weren't as clear as all that.

We eyed each other across the candle for a while. We were a long way from trusting each other right then.

"If you don't want to hear about Craghead, I'll go." She said. Then she smiled. "I suppose it's a compliment to have one's modification called 'unclear'." Sex and compliments – it's all they think about!

"What makes you so sure I want to even hear about this Craghead? I mean – why'd anyone want to meet *him*?"

"I heard you'd been asking. Circumspectly of course . . . but asking. . . . You don't give much away." That was a compliment too. She got out some factory-made cigarettes, offered them and I trusted her enough to take one. "Woodbine," a great old name, a rich rarity. I was liking her more every minute.

"Who told you?" I lit our fags with the candle.

"The Charcoal Burner, of course. We ... I employ him. He's a friend of mine. He told me all about you. How you came south so soon after that hoverer got itself burned ...?"

I put my hand on my knife. For a moment there it was in my mind to kill her. Woodbine or no Woodbine. She was bright, that was unusual for a Mod too. She must have sensed what I was thinking because she moved back in the straw and asked me who'd given me the papers and saved me from the Wardens anyway.

"Why should I betray you now?" she said. "I'd have been safer doing it at the inn! Easy too. Forget it, let's talk about Craghead."

"You work for him?" I took my hand from my knife. I had to admit she was logical. I was enjoying the smoke again.

"Well ..." she said. "That'd be telling."

"Suppose I don't want to tangle with this Craghead? Suppose I say I don't want to mess with his fight?"

"Ice Lover – you think you have a choice? You think you can refuse Craghead?" I let that go by, it was what I figured.

"OK. So tell me where to find him. I'll maybe talk to him – see if I like what I hear."

"Go on the way you're going about two or three days. Then turn south-west when you strike the Border. I'll pass the word. You'll be contacted. If you get asked, show this." She gave me one of those old plastic coins. A small green one. There must have been millions of them once. There weren't so many now.

Seeing the old money reminded me and I asked her what I owed her for the papers. I had some gold, it's the currency – that and ammunition. I don't like owing people for things – it means, sooner or later, you might have to do something for them and then you might not want to. She shook her head.

35

When she was at the door I asked her again who she was, if maybe I'd see her again. She didn't answer. She just shook her head and smiled a secret smile she had.

Then she asked me if I'd really been the guy who'd burned that hoverer and what happened to the Aliens in it. It was my turn. I could smile just as mysteriously as she could.

After she'd gone I thought I could hear voices outside. Then, before I could get a look, I heard an old-fashioned truck start up. It sounded like the Charcoal Burner's, but I'd seen him go north.

Later on I went and bought a sooty bottle off the Landlord and curled up with that. What I really wanted was a woman – but they'd all got fixed up by then. I was a bit depressed before the drink took hold, I was disappointed in Craghead's people – they shouldn't really need threats to bring me in. I wondered if it was really as good a hope as I'd thought it was.

I felt a bit better in the morning. The sun was shining and in the end I decided to do what I was told. Those people – the ones I'd met – Craghead's agents – they seemed to know what they were doing. They certainly seemed to know plenty about me. Craghead himself would have had to be pretty nasty and ruthless to get where he was, just the sort of guy who was needed. So I reckoned I didn't have a lot of choice and I'd better go on down south. Also I could still hope. Maybe it'd be better there – I mean, at least those guys were doing something, thinking about it at least – they had a leader after all, some kind of structure. When you thought about it they were all there was.

But I was still low. From all that good feeling and optimism of the morning before – all the certainty – I'd come to a sober pessimism. I was really on the downswing. I suppose it was seeing those Wardens and what they could do. Those weapons they had, that organization. That morning there didn't seem much a man could do against the Aliens.

36

Then there were the Mods. It'd been several years since I'd been in the Borderland, the Mods were a good deal worse than I remembered. People were more savage, poorer, more stupid than I'd thought possible . . . the whole thing was going downhill fast. Or so it seemed that black morning. Anyway, I did what I was told, I went south . . . I didn't have the energy not to.

As I went there were more and more ruins. Ruins . . . ruins all the way. Broken buildings, rusting machines and vehicles, old weapons and men's bones stained with mud, skulls, flaky and hanging on brambles like deserted crowns. There were great scars in the land, charred, prostrate forests and broken things between the secondary growth. Old plastic sadly blew and fluttered in the wind. When it started raining again that didn't help either.

There were old alien things too. Some, but not many. I saw a hoverer – just as they are today – rising out of the ground, impaled on a thrusting tree. One side was all ripped up, cockled and blown, what might have been inside had long since washed away. It seemed we managed to hit them sometimes. The trouble was it always took about fifty men to get one Alien.

Old Rutherford used to say that maybe we'd still have won if they hadn't come up with the modifications. We were on the verge of winning when they threw that in. Rutherford reckoned they worked with prisoners first. Put controls in and sent them against us. Then they got the Breeders going and the fighting modifications came after that, others too, then pretty soon it was all up with us.

Partly it's the chaos of the Defeat that makes us the way we are with each other, but mostly it's that you can never be sure if the other guy is carrying Aliens' controls or not. They used to send Mods against men with bombs in their stomachs and disease in their loins . . . some man you'd been fighting beside for weeks might suddenly shoot you in the back, or explode. So you can figure how things must have been in those last perimeters where men held out those last weeks. Since then there's

37

been two, perhaps three hundred years of barbarity and mistrust, you can see how important I thought Craghead could be.

If he could make order, establish discipline and law as well as killing a few Wardens then there was hope again. Maybe I could bend him that way, feed him thoughts – let him think they were his own ideas ... it could work.

But I was telling you about the Aliens and the Defeat. It was numbers they overwhelmed us with – our own numbers. When they got enough Breeders going it got so that Aliens were hardly ever seen. For the last fifty years or so men were mostly fighting men – or rather Mods, which really, though it's hard for me to say it, amounts to almost the same thing.

Another thing was that then, at the start of it, men were a whole lot softer. It was an effort then to shoot down your own kind. Men mutinied about it. It inhibited the weapons we used too – for a while I mean. Not towards the end, but it all worked against us – by the time we woke up it was too late and then there was that agonizing century of the Defeat, when we were pushed up to the Tundra and became few enough for the Aliens to almost tolerate.

The hell of it is that the Mods turned out to be better than we were. I don't mean those bastard Mods, the escapers and such in the Borderland but the pure ones. The ones the Aliens threw at us, like the millions they still have. They were specialized you see – better than us at particular jobs, like fighting and necessary things like that. Maybe we really had gone soft. Pretty soon we weren't though, everybody was the same – plain deadly – they had to be. We learned real fast – a lot of innate ability. Now Free Men are better than any of them.

By this time I'd turned south-west and about four miles on I came to the end of woodland. It looked like about the end of everything. The woods straggled off into utter desolation. The land went on, you could see last traces of old agriculture, the remembrances of fur-

38

rows and irrigation ditches, things like that. Sterile now
... dead, utterly dead.

The trees where I was were stunted, the further you
went the deader they were. All along that straggling
edge they were mixed up with strange Alien plants, a
kind of no-man's-land between us and them. In one or
two places the vegetation staggered out a bit further,
but beyond that there was no cover. I made my way
out in one of the tongues of woodland and sat there a
few moments, trying to make up my mind to go out
into the open.

I looked about and had a good long listen. It'd be
my luck to get caught in the open by a hoverer just
when I'd come so far. I was frightened – I admit it –
you must realize that this barren place was the *Border* –
and the Aliens were to the south of it.

There was only the noise of the wind. Just for a second I thought I heard a motor far in the distance – but
then I couldn't and there was just the wind again. The
girl had said I had to go that way so I told myself I
wasn't scared and took off across the mud. At least it
had stopped raining.

I got about twenty yards and my feet felt like they
were lead as the clay built up on my boots and legs. I
made it down into a gully that ran in the right sort of
direction and plodded up there. Right away I ran into
an old tractor. Rusted out it was – surrounded with red
stained soil and crisp flakes of rust. I guess the gully
was one of those country lanes they're always talking
about. There was nothing for me there so I trudged on.

I don't know what happened to that ruined bit of
country but it was like that for miles. Whatever it was
had been pretty final. Not even the smallest things grew
there – not even the toughest Alien plant.

A few hundred yards on I came to a ruined farm
place. A pile of the local stone and tattered plastic stuff.
Nothing organic survived about the place. There weren't
even any bones. I wondered if maybe it was some sort
of lingering radiation, a vibration maybe. I started wondering how long it would take to start to work on a

guy – what it might be doing to me! Perhaps some slow consuming thing was killing me by degrees – I found myself walking faster and faster. I steadied up, forced myself to go on more carefully.

I reckoned that vibration or whatever it was could only be the Aliens'. It's like they could work magic with living things ... modifying and destroying. It was almost as if they could get inside and mould nature to their intentions.

I climbed up out of the lane, left the farm place over my right shoulder and paused on top of a low rise. Maybe twenty miles north, well up in some hill country, I saw a great column of smoke. A massive slow column, rising straight up now that the wind had dropped for the evening. I started thinking about Craghead again. I turned and took a first sliding pace down the slope.

Then I saw the Wardens ... weapons glinting in their thick hands. They were about a hundred yards off and lower than me. They looked up at me. As I watched they started walking. I scrambled back over the top of the rise, dived and rolled down the other side. I sure got muddy. I got up and ran hard.

I cursed myself for a careless fool. I should have seen them – I would have, if I hadn't been looking over their heads and dreaming about that damn smoke. There were only three of them, I figured I might have a chance.

I came up the slope again about fifty yards left – by a big bare boulder that was there. The Wardens were coming up the slope towards where they'd seen me. They hadn't spread out at all. They'd never met anyone to make them careful. They thought it was all one big pushover.

As they came to the crest I crossed too, behind the rock in the other direction. I sprinted and slid in the mud to take them from behind.

I thrust up in their churned footprints and they were standing about twelve yards down the slope trying to figure where I might have gone to. Their eyes had just about followed where my footprints led – they decided

40

I must be behind the rock. The first brought up his weapon and shattered the boulder in hellfire and light.

I steadied my gun with both hands and let them have it. I hit the first square on the side of his carapace. One moment it was amber and translucent in the sunlight then it flared white and crazed about a black bloody bullet hole. I saw white silver bone shatter and explode into the air beyond him. Then I was shooting at the next. He went down in a flurry of mud. He wasn't dead – he kept trying to get up and I had to finish him later. The last Warden tried to swing his weapon round to get me. I shot him in the face. The bullet must have ploughed round inside his head because it churned out almost the same hole as it went in. Warden's skulls can be very thick, if you don't hit them just right – even with my pistol – that sort of thing happens.

That pistol was marvellous – it was the last design they ever made for Exploration Corps. Real good and compact. Beautiful – small-calibre triple velocity – the bullet was shaped to make a real vicious shock wave that could take your arm off if it missed you by less than a foot. If you weren't wearing armour that is. You've got to change the barrel every fifty shots. Old Rutherford gave me a supply of them, as well as the spare pistol.

When I'd finished the second Warden I sat down and tried to stop my hands shaking. I was really hit by it – I'd been so damn lucky again. I'd seen so much killing lately, ever since I came running south from the Tundra for safety and quiet. Now here I was, right on top of the Border and up to my neck in blood again. Here I was, in terrible danger, waiting for some hypothetical contact to turn up from someone I'd only heard of. Maybe those Wardens had given the Aliens the alarm. Perhaps a hoverer would show up soon – I wouldn't have much chance against one of them in the open. Maybe I should beat it back through the woods to the Tundra. I started wondering how long a guy could survive in this world anyway.

Then there was the whine and splutter of that old gasoline truck again. I knew it was the same one – one of the fan blades was out of pitch, so you could tell the sound.

The Charcoal Burner's blue truck slid out of a gully onto the flat bit where I'd first seen the Wardens. That girl again – the one who'd given me the papers – she was driving it. Not very well I thought. She waved up at me. She was laughing her silly head off. I wondered what anyone could possibly find funny.

"You should see your face!" she yelled. "You're bright green!" All right – so I'd been scared. You would have been too. "Come on down! Hurry up! I'll take you to Craghead."

I got up on my shaking legs and slithered and walked down the slope. I found I still had my gun in my hand, so I put it away.

"Come on! Come on! We can't stay here!" She slapped the seat beside her impatiently. I made it in the end. My muddy feet slipped on the truck's side and I cracked my shin on something hard. I felt good about the mud I brought into her nice clean truck.

The girl put fans in pitch and the truck lifted and moved forward. I sprawled back in the seat. I didn't have anything to say. I was depressed, I was thinking about a world where maybe there wasn't so much killing and you didn't have to live the way we did.

"Say something," the girl said at last. I was wondering why the hell she hadn't brought me down from the inn. It was a hell of a way to have walked when you didn't have to. Those Wardens too, I needn't have met them.

"I've got to admit you did well," said the girl after a few minutes.

"Yeah," I woke up. "Yeah . . . I did, didn't I?" I'd had enough of it all.

"You pass the test. Flying colours as they used to say."

"Test?"

"Well – you don't expect us – Craghead – to let *any-*

one in do you? We didn't even know if you were interested enough to come. We've got to be very careful about recruits."

"Test – it was a test? Those Wardens ... you put them there? How does that figure? Did Craghead control them?"

"Well – in a way." She was uncertain what to say. "In a sort of way ... we just let it out that there was a man going down on the Border."

"You told them?" I snarled. I thought I'd strangle the bitch!

"Don't take it like that. I knew you'd come through. You're the one that took that hoverer! Wardens are nothing compared with *that!* Anyway ... It was Craghead who insisted – and you don't argue much with him!"

We drove on in silence. Dusk came down, we rode on in that blasted land, wound through the twisting gullies, under the small dark clouds. I thought my black thoughts. After a while I went to sleep.

Hell! If she betrayed me again – I'd kill her sure! That'd be the first thing. Then I'd die fighting and that would be that. Who the hell cared either way? What did it matter? I felt comforted then. I went to sleep. It's awful ... it's the way it is now.

CHAPTER FIVE

I woke and we were in the foothills. It was morning and where we were the trees had just started their leaves.

It was like the Tundra never was. You could look back and see the Border – dark, blank, low-lying shapes ... dotted with ruined buildings and places where the soil had eroded away to bedrock ... heavy white channels of mist lying on it. But ahead ... ahead there were beech trees.

It was spring, the leaves were small, bright on the grey trunks and it was beautiful. Beech trees always look good anyway, after the Border they were paradise. At first there were some Alien plants as well – but they couldn't compete with the beeches. There were birds singing too.

When we were far enough into the woods we halted, the girl produced food and we had breakfast. We didn't talk much – we ate our picnic and looked at the trees. We didn't light any fire. By the time we'd finished, the sun was quite warm and the mists were rising up out of the fissured plain below us, burning off in amber and light. In a way that was beautiful too.

We droned on all through the morning. The truck was slow through trees. There were old vehicles we had to go round too ... the wasted shells of what was once, the wreckage of our old power. It was pretty depressing.

About midday the girl cut the motor and we stopped. That's the thing about gasoline motors, when you don't need them you stop them. They operate very slowly, not like the toroid-grav units, so it's not as inefficient as it sounds. It was all there was anyway.

We got out to stretch ourselves and snatch a bite while we could. While the girl got the food out I wandered down to have a look at a fighting machine with a hole in it. Right through it was – end to end – and a tree was growing on the mould inside. It twisted, light-seeking, to get out through the torn metal. There were a few scraps of paint inside but mostly it was all blistered and granular rust. It was another of those damn symbols my mind kept seeing. All the crumbled ruins of our glorious, long-gone yesterdays.

I said as much to the girl when she came back – she said what I needed was a drink and went to get the bottle. While she was gone I sat on a stump and listened to the silence. There wasn't even a bird in all that wild wood. I'd just started to wonder why not when there was a chink of harness behind me.

I whirled but it was too late. I was looking at a dozen grinning faces over horses' heads and gun muzzles.

I scowled back up at them, so they grinned at me some more. If I hadn't been thinking about that tank I might have heard their hooves in the mould. That was twice in a day I'd been caught out. Maybe I should go back to the Tundra, this civilized life was too fast for me.

"Have you gold, furry stranger man?" said the leader. "Have you gold about your person that might buy your life and gladden the hearts of poor Horsemen?" His horse moved about under him. It was a fine animal.

I scowled some more and raised my arms. I carried a throwing knife in my hood. I could take one with me, maybe warn the girl.

"Answer me, peasant! Show respect! Down on your knees!"

"I have a little gold, sir." Politeness costs you nothing. One thing, these guys clearly weren't Wardens. I didn't think they were controlled either. Controlled men don't have much sense of humour, these guys were laughing all the time. They were Mods though, but none of the grosser things – nothing that really showed. There were only a couple of carapaces and they'd been trimmed right back – I couldn't see any of those high-latitude pelts either, there were only a couple of guys who had anything like infra-red eyes. Maybe I could talk to them. If the girl could get in behind them with a gun . . .

45

"Ah . . . a wonder! An amazing thing how peasants always discover gold when asked!" They thought that was pretty funny too.

"Queer how it's always a *little* gold! Possibly they breed it in their trousers . . . take it out too young!" They were all laughing more than ever now. They were having a ball.

"So humane also . . . no attempt to harm us! No vulgar fighting for them! So ladylike!" That joker . . . he thought he was a great guy.

"Can I get my gold from my pack?" My gun was stuck in my belt. They'd not know about the one in my pack.

"Aye . . . we'll see the colour of your gold – that or your guts." That was a new one talking. I saw that he was really the leader, not that other guy.

"Lord, I will tell you without further search," said the funny one. "Yellow – like his rabbit's face! Have you fur on your back, peasant? Grey fur . . . and a small, puff tail?"

They really fell about at that. Do you know I once met a Mod with those sort of things? Think how that joker could have really hurt that guy's feelings!

The horses were shifting about, stamping. I had my pack open. I cocked and brought up my spare pistol all in one movement.

I didn't even have to aim properly. I put that shot six inches from the joker's face almost without looking.

His head burst off in a six-yard plume of blood and brains. Took it off easy – like blowing froth off beer. One thing, he did die happy.

Would you believe it but not one of them had been looking at me? Too busy laughing and controlling their horses. They were looking now. Frozen they were, their chins hanging. These guys hadn't been used to opposition either. Suddenly I felt good again. Bright-eyed and lively . . . cheerful and deadly . . . the best there was. With part of my mind I was hoping I wouldn't have to shoot someone every time I felt low.

"I'm a fierce, bad rabbit," I said. I centered my pistol

46

on the leader one and nobody moved. I went back and put my shoulders on the tank. We might have been there forever if the girl hadn't come up then.

"That'll ... that'll be enough," she said. She'd been running, her face was all red and she was breathing hard. She was frightened and angry as well. "Don't do anything!" she said when she had her breath back. "Don't anyone do anything."

I didn't look at her any more. I was watching the horsemen and wondering what in hell we were going to do.

"You shouldn't have done it, Ice Lover," she said. "These are some of Craghead's men. They were coming to meet us. I'd arranged it." It was all I needed. My luck again ... typical of the confusion that put us where we are.

It was a close thing. We must have stood there for five minutes just looking at each other. On one hand I knew I wouldn't last long if I used my pistol again, on the other hand Craghead's men didn't want to try anything with a gun like that on them. A wrong movement by any of us could have started it. I wasn't sure what the girl would do now either. I couldn't see any way out.

"What happened?" said the girl to me. "Why didn't you show that coin? It's the pass. Didn't they ask for payment?"

"Only for gold ... It was gold they asked for!" Wouldn't you know it? It was all confusion – all the way through. Just another example of the chaos. Symbolic in a way – what could you do?

"They should have acted civil! They should have asked for payment – like you said – not gold!"

"Fool! Now you've killed one of the Riders! One less to fight the Aliens! Always the killing! Only the one old answer to every problem!" She turned to the Riders. "You! You're just as bad! Payment! Payment was the word – not gold! How can we ever get organized if you don't follow the rules? How can we ever hope to fight the Aliens? You!" – she glared at the one they called "Lord" – "you're Craghead's son! It'll all be yours one

47

day. You should be an example. There'll be nothing unless you help build it. Now you've lost your father a
man! What'll he say to that?"

That was all it needed. Craghead's son! What a mess!
That Leader sitting there combing the joker's brain's out
of his beard was Craghead's son! Young Craghead!
How'd I ever get in now?

Young Craghead sat fidgeting on his saddle. He was
crimson in the force of the girl's speech, he kept his
eyes down. I couldn't figure if it was shame or anger.
One thing, I'd have to be careful about that girl, if she
could speak to Craghead's son like that, maybe she was
pretty important ... a real force there. I looked at her
with a new respect.

As the girl ranted on, young Craghead caught my
eye. He gave a little wink and a small, one-sided smile.
He rolled his eyes to the sky and I grinned back at
him.

"Aw, miss," said someone at the back, "that guy ...
he was so *quick* ... so sneaky – see how he keeps his
gun in his pack and that dummy on his belt!"

"Yes," she said. "He took you all. Took you like
babies. Couldn't you see he's from the Tundra? Those
furs should have told you that. Haven't you heard of Ice
Lover? That I was bringing him in – he's the one that
burned that hoverer! Now someone's dead and we've
got confusion! See Riders, see what you have done!"
She turned on me again. "You – Ice Lover – you put
that weapon of yours away. It's done plenty – got me
in enough trouble. How am I going to explain all this to
Craghead?"

In the end it was that we all agreed to trust each
other. It's easy when you try, we even shook hands. It
was as if the lashing the girl had given us had brought
us together ... made us feel like fools together – and
that was a sort of unity.

It turned out they weren't a bad bunch. I almost liked
the young Lord Craghead. He was pretty fierce and
dangerous – like a hawk. Young and hot – sensitive –
like a critical high explosive. Hair grew on his face in

irregular tufts. He had funny eyes too, one was black and one blue ... maybe one was bigger than the other, I couldn't tell. His beard had an orange cast of colour about it ... some of the Mods have some really curious features by now – what with two or three hundred years of uncontrolled breeding, all the genes confused and insane in the Borderland. As a matter of fact young Craghead was one of the least marked.

He came and sat with us in the truck. As we climbed in he winked again and whispered I wasn't to care too much about what had happened and what the girl had said.

"Don't you worry about killing poor old Kaid," he said when the girl drove off. "He was a no-count. Good for a laugh sometimes in winter. No one'll miss him. He wasn't even very funny really. Father won't worry about losing boring old Kaid. Didn't have the modification either. Sterile as well as stupid. Impotent ... just plain no-count!"

I said I was sorry all the same, but it had seemed like the thing to do at the time. I said I was worried about what the girl had said – that we shouldn't have confusions like that. He said he'd get round her OK.

"Don't fuss yourself. It was nothing. I'll tell father how the damn fool shouldn't have acted like that unless he had a gun on you . . ."

The girl drove on, picking a zigzag path through the woods, the horses could keep up quite easily with the speed we were making. I had a long talk with young Craghead. I told him most of what I knew about the Tundra and the country around the Charcoal Burner's. How there were fewer and fewer of us up there, how I hadn't seen a Free Man for years. I didn't tell him I was one, of course, and he didn't ask me about any modifications I had. That wouldn't have been etiquette – but I made sure he thought I was a Mod. He was curious about my gun – most impressed – but he was too polite to ask about that either.

Pretty soon we crossed out of the first line of hills and there was some cultivated country in a valley.

People have to eat, so there's a market for grown foods – not everyone can get the real canned stuff from the ice. The stuff the Aliens give out free to keep the people quiet doesn't taste of much and doesn't do you much good either. Makes you sterile they say, keeps you dozy and inactive, stupid – like the advertising they put out. Basically I guess it's just not nutritious enough to fight on.

Then we were out of the beeches and the hillsides we travelled were mostly bracken scattered with huge grey limestone boulders. Lichens and gorse grew there too, wiry-looking grass, sheep country – not much grows on limestone. In the valley there was a small river wandering on the flat farmland and a small settlement built amongst some old buildings. Young Craghead yelled some orders and some Riders set off towards them.

"Tithes," he said when I asked him. We went on while those guys were away and after a while they caught up with us again. They were laughing and galloping wild, they'd enjoyed themselves.

They'd had to burn a barn they said and one or two people had been killed before the peasants paid up.

"We protect them," said Craghead. "We defend them. Administer things. We're the organizers – we've got a right to treat them how we like. Fool 'em all the time we do ... they're only scum-peasants. They make plenty – we've got a right to it. Not men – not like you and me. And they've got some really ugly modifications down there – it's like those guys can't stop digging and planting things ... working."

I glanced at the girl. She didn't smile or anything – just kept looking ahead. It dawned on me that Craghead wasn't joking after all. When he turned to her she said he had it right and that everything was for the best, that the peasants expected it anyway and wouldn't understand better treatment. I couldn't figure whether she meant it or not. As time went by I found out that the nearer you got to Craghead's Underground the less you said what you were really thinking.

As the Riders came past I saw they were loaded

50

down with stuff they'd picked up. One guy had an arm-ful of white struggling hens. He pulled their heads off as he came, yelped with delight at each jerk and twist. Then he threw the dead birds away, behind him was dotted and littered with flapping white corpses and drifting feathers.

Another guy had a woman he'd grabbed off. He had her draped face down across his saddle. She sure was a Breeder, I never saw a backside like it! She seemed happy though, I suppose life with Craghead's Riders must have looked pretty good to a farm girl.

"Don't she wobble!" said young Craghead. "She sure is pink!" He slapped his thigh. He was delighted.

"Hiding in a sty!" shouted the man who had her.

"Pork!" screamed young Craghead. "Fat bacon!" We were all laughing. I mean, it was funny – you got to have your laughs! Then I saw the girl didn't think it was funny so I stopped.

Someone rode up and dropped a leather bag in young Craghead's lap. He suddenly got serious then and began counting the small pieces of silver. He enjoyed that too, kept licking his lips and starting again. He glanced up and saw me watching.

"Yeah," he said. "It's got to be right for my father." I saw the girl was looking at me again. While Craghead was still counting I turned to talk to her.

"They're a fine body of men," I said, to have some-thing to say. Mind, I meant it too. They were a hard bunch – quick and tough even if some of them weren't so bright. If anyone could take on the Aliens it was them. All they needed was someone to take them in hand. I just wished there were more Free Men, but I knew better than to say anything like that, not to anyone who was a Mod herself – certainly not a powerful one like she was.

"They're OK," she said. "They may do." She didn't really want to talk, so I shut up.

Then a hoverer came. We scattered into the moors, hid amongst the boulders. I was with young Craghead – in a fox lair. I had trouble deciding which smelled worse,

51

him or the fox. The hole wasn't very big – just a cleft between two leaning rocks.

The hoverer buzzed about a while like a big silver fly up there. I was shivering. Once I looked up and saw one of those blue spheres looking down back at me – where we were ... they couldn't have seen us. I was scared but so was young Craghead so he didn't notice. Hell, we had a right to be!

Then the hoverer went away up the valley and burned up that farm. For fun maybe. I mean, there was nothing there worth much, nothing really, nothing to burn up. Unless they had a policy to make sure people had to eat more of those special foods of theirs. They burned the crops too and I thought how little protection that tithe seemed to buy.

"Good thing you didn't take that hoverer," said young Craghead when it was gone. "Not so near home, I mean." He thought a moment. "I couldn't have stopped myself ... I'd have tried ... if I had your gun I'd have taken it!"

He had a hope. It was never nearer than a mile except that time it came over us. Up there buzzing and circling ... ugh! I can't stand even the thought of flies. I doubt if I could have shot straight enough – even if my gun could damage a hoverer at that range. So I just grunted. I'd lose nothing letting the Riders think my gun and me were that good. It'd be easier to be friendly with these people if I frightened them some.

CHAPTER SIX

WHEN evening was coming on, as the mists began to come in the valleys, we came up onto a broad plateau and saw Craghead's place ahead – or rather the smoke of it rising up out of the mist. The girl told me what it was, but by the time we got near the mist had closed right down and got to be a fog. Young Craghead and the girl became vague presences sitting next to me, it was as thick as that.

We still went on though. Quicker and quicker as the Riders got more excited. I saw after we'd come in on an old road – like the one under the Aliens' highway. All cracked and broken – concrete – the old stuff. It seemed to have started suddenly – come up from nowhere, it was rough but it kept us from getting lost. It must have been splendid once. There were still some unbroken areas, but they were tilted and canted – there wasn't anywhere that was level. I thought maybe it was some sort of ceremonial drive and that was why it started so suddenly. The truck bottomed sometimes and you could hear brambles tearing on the skirt.

Fresh Riders loomed enormous out of the fog. There was the levelling of wet glinting weapons, shouted challenges, then jokes and laughter. One man leaned into the dim lighting of the truck. I saw beads of mist on his beard as he spoke to young Craghead. He nodded respectfully to the girl, then took his head out and we went on.

The man that had the farmer Breeder was beating her across her bare buttocks, using her like some fleshy, rounded drums. She squealed, she was delighted, she was loving it.

Everybody was happy. Some guys began to fire in the air. The fog flared and echoed with the reports, pretty soon the spent bullets were coming down like hail. More men came with oily smoking torches, there was singing and someone started to play a bugle.

The guards guided us in. There were earthworks first, twisting rampart labyrinths, set about on top with sharp stakes, dark mazeways lit with guttering pitch torches, twisting left and right, confused and muddy underfoot.

Later there were more stakes with people's heads on them and a couple of gibbets with hanged men. I thought I saw a maggot on the face of one of them – but maybe that was a trick of the light.

In a clamour of shouted passwords, jokes and obscenities we reached the main gates. That Mod was still beating his Breeder but she'd stopped squealing now. Maybe it had gone numb. Craghead said maybe he'd beaten her brains out.

There were torches and bonfires all around us now, the whole fog glowed with light, uneasy orange, figures moved, grotesque shadows shifted and danced. Maybe some of the guards had the infra-red, or the bat modification, I couldn't see any way through it all but they brought us quickly in, straight across the confusing mystery of that light and fog-lost forecourt to the gates.

I had an impression of a vast wall, forty feet high maybe, tall and disappearing into the fog. It was made of great stones, plastered between with clay and whitewashed. Places were bare, the clay lay where it had fallen in smooth eroded piles, mingled with whitewash flakes at the wall's foot. It was ancient, really *old*, all marked with time and history ... a century or two of falling rain.

Then there were iron and wood gates, heavy with rust ... thick black old grease at the hinges. The guards pushed them back with crowbars and we drove into a deep chasm, unroofed, right through the wall.

There were embrasures on either side, so that they could shoot down on you, I never saw a worse place to get caught with a grenade.

The floor ran first down then up. There were more torches in there and maybe less fog. Where it was lowest there was a wide pool of what smelled like sewage.

Water or something flowed in at the far side and out the way we had come. Our truck blew up clouds of stinking spray on either side, the Riders cursed us jovially as we passed.

The shouting and fooling was louder than ever in there, all echoing against the walls. Some fool started firing his gun and the horses clattered and pranced, bodies glinting and steaming in the torches. There was a scream as a ricochet knocked a man from his saddle, then laughter as he scrambled to get up in the water. The truck went right over him, I saw him struggle out of the spray behind us. He was OK, bright blood ran on his shoulder from the bullet, but he was OK. I saw him spitting out a mouthful of the dirty water.

Man, the whole place *stank*. It was as bad as flies. I hated to be closed in with all that fighting and scrambling. I got a headache and started to feel mad ... killing mad ... I could hardly breathe. Then something snapped and I was miserable – not mad any more, just crushed with the sadness and sorrows of it all. Times like that and you could cut my throat and if I noticed I'd probably thank you. Mean and evil ... all that stinking and stupid, raucous humanity came crushing in on me, I couldn't keep from crying. Then it all receded away and I was somewhere else, it left me grey and all washed out.

We went through another gate and into the open again. That wall must have been fifty yards thick there. Just to impress the peasants, I guess, it wouldn't have kept the Aliens out, not for five minutes. It was cold white fog again out there but it was better than that gate. We drove on a while and there were lighted doorways.

It was just another of those small dirty villages that people called towns and cities. Why for God's sake anyone would put a wall round it I couldn't see. I couldn't even see that great column of smoke that marked the place. Lost in the fog – I suppose. When we got into the village I started thinking how great it'd be to be up on the Tundra again without all these people. I knew what

55

it was to love ice then ... that's me all right – Ice Lover.

There were women and children to greet us. All Mods – or Breeders – lived in those small lean-to huts they did – came out like flies in the sun to see the return of the splendid Riders. All dirty and unkempt – filthy – they'd let themselves go the way Mods did sometimes. Some of them didn't look as if they had any humanity in them at all. They were far gone beneath that ... but how can you expect a Mod to respect himself? That accounted for a whole lot of crooked breeding – people just didn't care. It's those beastly Aliens, I thought, it's all their fault. They did it to us – I wanted desperately to kill an Alien right then.

Someone caught my arm and told me that we couldn't get to see Old Craghead right then – that we'd have to wait till the next day. Said to amuse myself in town while I was waiting.

There was an inn handy so I tagged on behind young Craghead's boys and had a few with them. Hell I told myself, I'd made it after all, I'd made Craghead's enclosure at least, so I'd celebrate.

As soon as I could without offending anyone – it sure wasn't a place to insult a man, I never saw so many weapons in one place – I bought a bottle and beat it out of there. I was a drag on the party anyway – I sure wasn't in the mood for the pleasures they had in mind.

I wondered what had happened to the girl. She'd got out of the truck on the other side from me and I hadn't cared then when I lost sight of her. Now I wanted someone to talk to there wasn't anyone, they were all Mods.

I stumbled up the black, rutted street, I talked to a dog but it tried to bite me. Then I talked to a kid but it couldn't. Surely kids should be able to talk before they're ten? Like I keep saying the Aliens had done some pretty rotten things to us – and they're still working at it, what's more. Man ... we *had* to do *something* about it! If we could.

In the end I found the truck and it seemed like a good place to curl up with my bottle. There was a roof for one thing, but the girl was in there and threw me out.

56

Said she was sleeping there – and I couldn't. Said she had plenty of her drugs left and to forget it.

So I staggered off up the dungy and unpainted street. Human dung is so much worse than any other kind. Then I found a shed stuffed with hay that was fairly clean and tried to climb inside my bottle there. I got to sleep after a while – in spite of the noise from the inn. There's nothing worse than a riot when you're not in the mood.

Two hours later a woman showed up and said young Craghead had sent her. I appreciated the thought but she was a Breeder of course and she had woken me so I was a bit short with her. She started to cry then so I gave her my bottle, she emptied it and that seemed to satisfy her.

I'd had too much booze to be any good to her anyway. When she'd shut up I got to sleep again. Then that dog that tried to bite me came and curled up at my feet. I guess he was maybe sorry about what he tried to do, it was something.

In the morning the girl came and beat me over the head until I woke. I sure had a headache. I swear that booze'll kill you in the end. The sun was too bright as well.

"Come on! Come on slob!" shouted the girl. "Snap out of it! Craghead's waiting!" That Breeder who came in the night, she had her arms around me so I kicked her off and made it out into the hurtful sunshine.

When my head had finished exploding and I didn't figure I was going to die anymore I saw things weren't quite so bad as I'd thought the night before. That nasty little village then was only part of the story, even the people looked better in the bright morning. Maybe it was the pill the girl gave me to eat, after a while I could even take the sun. Then she showed me where there was a trough of running water and I splashed about in that some and took a longer look around.

The Enclosure was big – much bigger than I'd thought last night. Oval, maybe two or three miles long, perhaps half as wide, enclosed by the wall. It was a meeting place for those old roads, maybe they went on outside the walls. There were some indigo and green pines – some solitary but mostly in several large stands. The pink and silver trunks looked real good against the pale sky of that morning. The grass was a particular lush sort of green, there were fine horses hobbled and grazing ... there were some fat sheep too, here and there, amongst heavy concrete rectangles which punctuated the turf.

There were even some quite good houses set back from the village – they had glass windows set off with painted woodwork, nice things like that. There wasn't a cloud in the sky, all that fog had gone, even that early sun struck warm in your face, there were milk cows and a dairymaid. Suddenly I felt good. I guess it was partly that pill – it was better than booze.

The girl led me down the village street and up onto a cracked forecourt sort of thing. Ahead, up at the far end of the Enclosure you could see the splendid column of smoke I'd seen from the Border. It piled up and up in the calm air, beyond that there were blue-green woodland distances. It was good to feel the fresh air on my face. I was ready for anything and said so. I said I'd take on a whole army of Wardens if I had to.

"Good," said the girl. "Now we'll see how you make out with Craghead." At last, after all that long search, after all that journey I'd made it to the man whose name had brought me. It'd been a struggle and often I'd almost turned back – but here I was at last and I was glad.

"Come on then – let's go!" I was excited. I tried not to show it, but I knew I did. That Craghead – he was *great* – he was *famous* and I sure wanted to see him. Maybe it was that pill, I don't often feel like that. The girl smiled that secret smile of hers and off we went.

On the other side of the good houses, hidden by some pines, there was a hole. It was where the water in the gate came from, it bubbled out of an iron-bound wooden pipe there – into that trough I'd washed in the other end of. A fair sort of stream – kind of pulsing it was, like a heartbeat but slower. An animal quality, I wasn't so sure it was so clean now either.

The hole itself was pretty big, thirty or forty feet across I'd guess, lined and round. A few feet down the concrete gave way to square cream bricks, much eroded – and then, where they had fallen away, to living rock. There was a limestone parapet round the top and worn steps leading to a platform a few feet down the shaft. There were some plants clinging down there, but mostly it was pretty clean. Far, far below in the near dark I caught the glint of lights, there was the remote murmur of voices and of falling water.

Maybe a dozen guards stood around the parapet, they quickly let us down the steps onto the platform when they saw the girl. Two of the guards stepped forward to help her even, but she waved them away.

A rod led up the shaft and passed through a loop of iron strapped to the parapet. Someone had daubed great handfuls of grease on it there, a couple of yards down the rod gave way to two heavy parallel timbers, there were newish-looking rungs driven through to form a sort of narrow ladder.

When we were on the platform one of the guards shouted down the shaft, there was an echoed acknowledgement and the rod and ladder began to move slowly up. When maybe twelve feet stuck up it stopped, paused, then began to travel back down.

"Come on! Do like me!" The girl had stepped onto the descending ladder. "Come on down!"

"Down there?" I said. It looked dark there – hell of a way to fall. Warm fetid air hit my face ... humid – just the sort of place flies might breed. Thousands of them ... all clinging to the walls ... moving there – breeding.

"Come on!" The girl disappeared with the ladder as it moved down. "Do what I do!" Then when I hesitated: "That rabbit fur tickling your back?"

So I had to go. I stepped onto the ladder. I sure got cured of those pills then.

The thing didn't stop. As soon as I got to where the

59

girl was the whole lot began to move back again and I only just had time to get off. There was a ledge there – on either side of the ladder, she was on one side, I was on the other.

"There," she said. "Not so bad, was it?" Then, as the ladder stopped and began to move down again she stepped onto it and was gone. I had the idea by then and followed her down on the next stroke. The rhythm developed, each throwdown was identical – except that the platforms seemed to get smaller and smaller ... and more slippery too. There were staples to hang onto and I sure did.

Time and time again we made the movement. Each stroke took us a little further from light and air, a little deeper buried. By the time I hit the bottom I reckoned we were maybe a hundred and fifty feet down and plenty lucky to make it.

It still went down. That hole looked like it went on forever. The ladder we were on gave way to an iron rod again where we got off and went through the metal grid that was the floor of the shaft. Below the grid it got wider and there was a big wheel which was cranked up to the moving ladder. The wheel was a sort of treadmill filled with animals and sweating men – some were driving the animals but mostly they were tramping the mill and were driven themselves. There were torches down there and the lash of whips.

The stench was terrible, the walls ran water ... there were more men and animals waiting their turn on the wheel. The floor down there was another grid and below that again, far away, lit by falling torch sparks, I caught the sullen gleam of water. I thought I saw excrement floating down there and what looked like a corpse turned sluggishly in some mysterious current.

"Come on!" said the girl and she led off down a tunnel that ran horizontal from where we were. There were others leading left and right, they'd been built up with bricks and rubble – maybe the stuff they'd taken out when they widened the shaft for the wheel. I went willingly after the girl, the smell there was real bad.

The tunnel was pretty good, about twelve feet wide and seven high. It was concrete on the walls with only the occasional place where the lining had fallen away and you could see rust-stained reinforcement. There were one or two places where the walls were still covered with a thick grey plastic stuff, but almost all of that was gone. The floor was much the same and those square pipes that put the water on the surface led on the way we were going. They were bracketed to the wall about every six feet – it was a neat job, the wood was new-looking. I thought maybe it was a contemporary thing – not just something else left over from the bright past. There was hope in that. Maybe someone was making things – someone who'd got hold of a pump, found out how to use it – then maybe made the pipe. It was a hopeful thing – somebody still had the energy to start to do something. There were bits of fungus starting to grow on the wood. Even the new stuff was getting old.

There wasn't much light. Just once in a while there was one of the old ones still working and the girl had a torch she'd picked up somewhere. She knew where she was going so I followed dumbly on, hoping and trusting and cursing. I felt like a little dog.

There were places every so often which had been crudely built over and a low arch left that you practically had to crawl through. There were usually guards on the other side to knock your brains out if they had a mind to or if you didn't have the password.

"It's a sensible arrangement," said the girl as we struggled through one place. "The Underground is well protected. Any attack and they knock the pins out of the link on the treadmill and the whole ladder goes down through the floors like an arrow. Right down into deep water. Take anything on the ladder with it. Over a hundred and fifty feet – we've plumbed that far . . .

"All the corridors are fixed to blow. If the Wardens or even the Aliens ever really press home an attack the charges will be exploded. No one'll penetrate then. Take a lot of attackers out too – with any luck."

"What about the guys inside?" I said. I mean . . .

they'd be dead too – but slower. The girl said how there were maybe one or two hundred secret exits to Craghead's warren – that the whole of the limestone was riddled with them. She said it was planned that the men would escape and be hard to catch in the woods. They'd rally to Craghead and fight on from hiding. She said how they'd sure thought of a simple thing like not getting caught in their own trap.

That tunnel – corridor – was getting hotter all the time. Soon there were wreaths of steam hanging about the place. There was a smell of hot metal too. As we walked on it got less dark and then, up ahead, I could see plenty of light.

The way looked clear so I speeded up and pretty soon I was walking right beside the girl – maybe even a little in front. I was fed up with walking behind a Breeder Mod – it wasn't dignified.

It was dangerous though. In one place there was a cracked sort of chasm where the floor dropped away to nothing and the girl only just saved me so I started walking behind her again.

The corridor was lower now, we had to go through more and more of the low arches and in several places it was fixed so they could shut down great grids like the ones across the shaft. The girl kept showing me places where there were explosives – mostly neocordite out of ammunition, old rocket fuel, stuff like that – to bring down the roof and worse. She could see how it upset me to know they were there, but she kept right on telling me.

Those lights up ahead were getting brighter and brighter. I kept wondering what sort of place it was that Craghead had – maybe, considering that light, he wasn't very much modified. Maybe he was almost human.

CHAPTER SEVEN

THE girl went on feeding me all that guff about those escape routes when we suddenly came into a wide and brilliantly lit space.

It was a double room – equal spaces on either side of the corridor. Symmetrical, white with ceramic bricks with raw places where walls had been torn down to make more space. There were lights and more lights there and two great engines, one on either side.

They filled the whole of those rooms. Thirty or maybe forty feet high, reaching from floor to roof. Steam had something to do with them, steam and fire.

There were strong furnaces underneath, guys with long shovels kept belting charcoal and wood into them. Then there were great steam-leaking upside-down bucket shapes above that and I couldn't see any more for steam. Above the steam there was like a huge seesaw thing that worked slowly – but with great power – up and down. There was a flue arrangement that disappeared into the roof where there was another shaft like we'd come down. A rod from that seesaw beam worked down again into a cylinder arrangement – that square pipe we'd been following led from there.

The girl murmured something about pumping engines and hurried on past so I didn't have time for more than a glance. But I saw a guy up on that great seesaw beam thing pushing grease into that slow grinding bearing up there. I remember thinking how careful he'd have to be about working on a thing like that. Then I briefly saw another guy on the floor telling the greaser what to do. I didn't figure it for a while, but there was something about that guy on the floor ... something. It nagged at me, there was something I maybe ought to remember. There was so *much* I didn't understand.

Then – almost suddenly – we were through a last

short darkness, past guards with funny infra-red eyes and into the hall of Craghead. Into what really was his Underground.

Now ... that, *that* was something else. A big place – four or maybe five hundred feet long – more across ... you couldn't really tell, it all tailed off into remote and uncertain darkness.

There were thick columns and complicated concrete tracery – I could see that – and a hot press of people shadowed and thrown up by firelight deep in the hall. But you couldn't penetrate to the ends of the place, they ended in dark and smoky mystery.

In the middle – I reckoned right in the dead centre – there was that great fire. Logs, whole trees burned there, smoke and flames leapt sparky ways up into the cowled shaft above. That shaft was exactly like the other two I'd seen, except that it was blackened and the flame had eroded the crisp edge that should have been visible at the far side of the cowl. Up further it was caked deep with soot, really black ... grown into fantastic shapes with the deposits of years.

I guess that was how they kept the air fresh down there – circulating it in the energy of the massive convection of that fire – sucking in fresh air at the entrances, then spitting it hot and exhausted up that great vent. That was where that massive tower of smoke that stood up on the surface came from – that great beacon I'd seen so long ago.

The girl left me. She said she'd approach Craghead, that I was to stay where I was until she came back for me. She disappeared into the crowd and I had time to look around.

The walls I could see were all hung with tapestries and drapings. Some were very beautiful, trees and buildings, great men on them. They'd been made of bright silks but they were old now, darkened and destroyed with dust and smoke. To my left and right I could see how the space had been divided up, some sort of semiprivate quarters made off with tent divisions, where some of the people could do whatever it was in privacy. On the wall where we'd come in the drapes were thrown back to make the entrance and you could see big irregular shapes painted onto the walls there. Big ragged shapes – paintings that didn't represent anything, if you can believe that – maps they were called, someone told me.

It was hot in that hall – hot and dark. The servants kept the fire up too and they were always running about with buckets of water or something, people had to be drinking all the time in that heat.

There were a lot of really old people there when you looked. They weren't all fresh young hawks like young Craghead's men. Scraggy round the neck – a lot of them ill or dying – in that quick decline of rot and decay that comes so suddenly to Mods. There were women too, all Breeders that I saw, but I didn't see any children. The Breeders were all dressed in heavy high-necked robes, laden down with gold and jewels. In the heat it must have been unbearable. Sweat ran on their smooth white painted faces, washing the colour away and revealing the mosaic tints beneath, then over the shaved eyebrows and into the black-rimmed eyes. It's amazing what people will do for fashion and to hide their piebald Mod skins. They were very beautiful.

Everybody seemed very conscious of fashion in Craghead's court – I guess it was maybe just about all some of them had on their minds. One good thing was that furs were in fashion so I could keep on my coat and still pretend I was a normal Mod.

Then the girl came and said we were to go up and talk to Craghead. We went forward and started to shove through the press nearer to Craghead's throne. I listened to what people were saying as we passed but I didn't learn much, it didn't seem to have much meaning. It was like they were trying to show each other how bright they were and to see how often they could work in any words that happened to be fashionable. "New concepts" or "the flux and interchange of ideas" they called it. I said something about it to the girl and she said it worried her too. She said that those guys wouldn't know an idea if they had one and that if something didn't happen soon – something *real* – like an attack on or maybe by the Aliens, then the whole thing would die on its feet. She said that some of them hadn't been on the surface for ten or maybe twenty years and they hadn't much idea of what reality was like there – so to be careful what I said. According to her the catchwords were just random, they didn't mean a thing – but she said not to say that or they'd pretend to think I was old-fashioned and stupid. I wasn't sure if I cared what they thought, they were just a bunch of Mod monsters – it wasn't like they were Free Men.

Then I thought that they had the power so maybe I'd play along. She saw what I was thinking and said that that was what everybody did, but not to say anything like that either.

One interesting thing was that the servants that worked the fire were Wardens, or had been. You could see great gaping holes in their carapaces where they'd had the communicator burned or torn out. They weren't too bright of course, even by local standards, but they had thick skins against the heat and they sure did their job.

I saw the fire was built on another of those grids across the continuing shaft, every once in a while someone would tip a tree or so down from above and it would come crashing down in a shower of soot to explode into the blaze. Ash and stuff just fell through into the water below, when you were close to the fire you could hear it spitting and hissing in the darkness there. I thought I could smell meat cooking too but it turned out to be some prisoners they were roasting. Once in a while the servants would throw water over them to stop their clothes actually burning. I wondered what metal that grid was to stand up to that fire so long.

Then the people parted and we came to Craghead himself. And boy, was he something.

Old. The first thing about Craghead was that he was *old*. Ancient as some bleached, scoured bone washed up on some long-dead seashore ... some long-dead tree up

66

on the Tundra. He was absolutely hairless ... the skin had a white translucent quality ... but when you looked it was slightly blemished into small mosaic pieces of tiny variations of that old pale plastic colour. He looked like if you held a flame behind him he'd glow.

He was all dressed up in rich old things – a fur-lined sort of khaki jacket scattered with brown and black shapes. He had thick armour padding underneath, he was bound up with belts and pouches shaped to fit his chest and back. His legs were wrapped in old trousers, he had boots on his feet – the rich old sort that lace and clip as far as the knee. About his shoulders there were the remains of what I thought must be one of the personal grav units they used in ancient times. Over all, but thrown open, he had thick furs, to be in fashion I suppose, they fattened him too – made it so he wasn't too puny.

All around the dais there were charcoal braziers. It was unbelievably hot. Craghead liked it so. He had a carapace in his thin old hands. As he turned it the heavy skull clunked and slipped inside. When he saw we had come, he put it down and picked up his great helmet and put that on.

He lived in a kind of shelter up on his dais. The throne was set there in a sort of open-ended tent made from that old kind of netting stuff supported on a white-metal-tube structure. There were bits of cloth still hanging on the netting and the whole thing was inches thick with that black gritty dust of the place. There were a dozen guys with guns who were guards and another, younger guy who had some kind of stringed instrument and a set of reed pipes which he was softly playing.

When we got before the dais the girl walked up and stood behind Craghead. I don't know what she said, but she stooped and whispered to him and he turned to me.

Those eyes looked down at me from under the swept-out edge of his helmet. A battered webbing chinstrap hung beside his thin mottled face, a few shreds of netting clung to the high dome of the helmet, Craghead's eyes shone red and amber in the firelight . . . like a dog's. I wondered just what his modifications were. Apart from the secondary arms and things like that it's sometimes very hard to tell what they are in the very old.

"SILENCE! Silence for the Lord Craghead!" A fat guy with a loud voice came forward and was shouting to wake the dead. "The Lord Craghead, Master of Thunders, Lord of Fires, Bull Roarer and North Star, Poseidon and Dweller of Deeps! He speaks!"

The people stopped shifting and stood still, their conversation and shouting softened and died. Craghead leaned forward. His teeth were perfect . . . maybe they were the old false sort.

"So you are this Ice Lover of whom there is so much talk. My good girl, my own advisor, has told me of you. A good man and sudden fighter seemingly . . .?"

"I am Ice Lover – I do what I can."

Suddenly people had stopped breathing. Eyes stared at me, horrified.

"The correct address is LORD CRAGHEAD!" That fat guy was shouting in my face again. His breath was rotten. "Show respect for your betters!" It looked like the thing to do, so I stopped staring at Craghead and murmured sómething that might be taken to sound like "Lord".

It was a nasty moment. Craghead sat rigid. I could feel his eyes boring right into me. The girl was whispering to him again. I stood there and felt scared. The silence seemed to go on and on. You couldn't hear anyone breathe . . . just the noise of the fire and the hiss and splash of falling embers.

Then, unexpectedly, Craghead smiled. I heard the breath come out behind me and the people there moved a little. It was OK again – I believe some of them were even glad for me.

"We don't expect too much from you, Ice Lover. A Bumpkin . . . a barbarian from the north," he said. "Living up there lonely . . . without contact with polite company, without education. The Lord Craghead can afford to be *magnanimous* with such!"

"Craghead the *Magnanimous*!" shouted the girl. The people took up the word and soon they were practically dancing to it. For a while some thought it was "magnificent" and shouted that, but they soon had it right. I even heard one guy say that he thought roast pork was magnanimous!

The girl mouthed that I should thank him and I did. I called him "magnanimous" too. Well ... what the hell!

"We will find duties suitable for your talents, Ice Lover, there is much opportunity for one that kills so well."

Then he got down to important things like practising how to pronounce "magnanimous" right. He was delighted with the new word. I reckon the girl gave it to him and that it saved my life. For a while I was forgotten, left standing there while people got back to their business. After a while Craghead remembered me and called me up to him.

"We will show you our attributes," he reached up and grabbed my shoulder, pulled my face down to his. "Honour for you after your long journey, Ice Lover, your long search for us. They shall not say virtue is unrewarded in our court!" He turned away, still holding my head down. "Guards! Be near us!" then he leered back to me. "Our holy collection. The relics of past power and holiness long gathered by our dynasty. And we will show you all, Ice Lover!"

I thanked him. "A great privilege, Lord Craghead," I said. And I meant it too. It *was* a privilege. Craghead's regalia was the central myth – the holiness and symbol of the man. Everybody knew of it, very few had seen it, but it was the form of the promise that one day we would surely return and rise again to the promise of our own land.

"Come on! Come on!" He led the way through the netting at the back of the dais. Men ran to hold the curtains away for him, when the men were slow he beat at the curtain with his stick. The dust came showering down.

"We are here, Lord," said the girl. "Come, Ice Lover! Come see the things of rare promise!"

"Lord, thank you for your magnanimity!" I said and scurried after them.

We went through the back and it was pretty dark there but the guards had torches and walked on either side so you could see fairly well. That guy with the pipes came too, whistling quietly to himself in the darkness.

"Give us a hymn," said Craghead. "A psalm ... something righteous!" The guy started playing and singing something about marching and fighting into a promised paradise, but I didn't really understand it all.

A few minutes and we came between two ranks of columns, like an aisle. They were enormous, very mysterious, rounded in the torchlight, scores of them, placed maybe six feet apart, leading into dark and holy distance. You couldn't see the tops of them, they were too high, but the bases were spread, like the flights on an arrow. They were all on trolleys, so that, maybe, they could be moved. They were very noble, somehow virile and strong in that dark place.

"These are our father's weapons." Even Craghead kept his voice low in that place. "Bombs that would reach a great distance. We have lost their art, but one day ..."

There were some guys who were cleaning the pillars, polishing them, you could see the metal they were made of. The men mumbled to themselves as they worked, prayers I suppose ... that was understandable. It was a very holy place.

Then we were through there and out into a wider space, passing stacked and streamlined shapes, some flighted and some not. Some were polished and cleaned and others were covered with that thick black dust of the Underground.

"Napalm," said Craghead. "The old, old magic and beauty of such ancient names. Projectile ... weapons system ... ten-thousand-pounder ... antipersonnel ... the glory of these relics! Some, alas, we cannot order

70

cleaned or painted. We know well the dangers of laying the sinful hands of our time upon them. History would be angry and deal us death. Do not walk near the bombs that weep, Ice Lover." He led the way carefully through stacked piles of explosives, the hanging rich belts of machine-gun ammunition garlanding the squat bombs. He showed us the plastic-packed charges for the big guns, the huge separate shells . . . spare barrels . . . each weapon set about with its own strange, silent eyes.

There were vehicles too, all polished, clean, ready-looking. Trucks like the girl's with small rocket projectors, guns and things like that mounted on them.

"These we can use," said Craghead. "Some we have already moved out, they are similar to trucks already available . . . when the time comes . . ."

They could too, they could use them, they were simple enough. There were tools as well. Metal to work and the machines to work it with. Welders and spanners, drills and those cylinders of gas that Old Rutherford had valued so much. He'd go mad with gear like that, there'd be nothing he couldn't do with it.

And then it hit me. Old Rutherford! That guy I'd seen directing things on those pumps! His back had been turned and I'd only glimpsed him through the steam but it was Old Rutherford. I knew like I know I'm a Free Man! It was Old Rutherford!

CHAPTER EIGHT

I STOOD there with my mouth open and Craghead kept right on walking through and showing us his stuff. I got left in the dark there with a stupid grin all over my face.

It was wonderful! That old polar bear hadn't got him after all. Rutherford was still alive! I should have known it – take more than a polar bear to kill him! The only other Free Man I ever knew for sure. It was great to know he was still alive and making things! I bet he made those engines with his teeth and bare hands for some great Rutherford purpose he had in mind. After all the rest it was great to know there was a thinking man about.

Craghead broke into my thoughts. He'd halted a few yards ahead, now he was waiting for me. Tiny frowns began to move on his forehead. I hurried to catch up, I did my best to concentrate, to look interested.

"Have some ... fill your pockets!" Craghead had stopped by a row of great dishes filled and overflowing with small glinting things. Small-arms ammunition it was, all there – all sorts and sizes – from the smallest to the biggest. Copper and brass and nickel ... some of those plastic ones too. "Go on – take some! Have as many as you want!" He scooped his hands through them, the ammunition rattled and poured in a small cascade through his fingers. He started handing them out like candy. To be polite I took some, but they weren't a bit of good for anything that I could see, gold and silver were all they valued in the Underground.

But what I was thinking about was how I could get back and talk to Rutherford – make sure if it really was him. Somehow there were things that gnawed in the back of my mind about the Underground – small things maybe ... but things that weren't right. Rutherford would know the answers. Then Craghead was showing us trays and banks of small things, radiation grenades mostly.

All spread out like on a fruit stand they were, all exhibited there like goodies. I dragged my thoughts back.

Radiation grenades could really be useful. They yielded a short sharp burst of X rays and worse that killed everything inside about ten feet. If you're fifteen feet away then what you get is a nasty dose of sunburn and maybe radiation sickness – maybe blinded if you don't shut your eyes or get behind a wall or something. Those grenades – they last too, made to survive storage – I got Craghead to give me a couple. He didn't really want to part with them – they were still useful, not like the ammunition – he didn't like to give anything like that away. I let on how magnanimous I would think him if he let me have a couple. So he nodded and I put a dozen of the little bombs in my pocket.

"We are indeed magnanimous," said Craghead, proud as Punch. "You see how *worthwhile* is our court!"

"A privilege to work close to you, Lord. To be part of your *worthwhile* team!" Maybe "worthwhile" would be the next word. The girl whispered it had been "team" last week and I was too late with it.

But I was worried. This place could easily be fatal. Not only in case Craghead turned nasty and had you killed – that was a big risk – but all those explosives piled up there, they were pretty frightening too

All those sweating bombs – Rutherford had told me once what that meant! All those dangerous explosives . . . tons of the stuff all ready to blow. I mean – it only needed the wrong touch. Just one small explosion and it'd all go up – straight up about five hundred feet I guessed . . . there wouldn't be much left and that'd be in small pieces.

I wondered if Rutherford knew about it. He might maybe know some way to make it safe – or safer. Anyway, I didn't mention it to Craghead, he wouldn't have understood. Probably have taken any thought like that as cowardly and disloyal. But it was dangerous . . . those piled warheads began to look like giant flies' bodies lying there . . . it was like living in a gun barrel.

"It is not all," said Craghead proudly. "Not all our

73

potent glories. Come, follow us and we will show you all the holy mysteries of our heritage."

We all murmured something about "worthwhile magnanimity" and followed on. The quicker we got through this and out the better – the quicker I could get to talk to Rutherford.

We walked on in our interlocking spheres of torchlight. We were crossing a vast empty space now, there was nothing – no ordnance, no walls, no nothing. Only dust, beaten down into the path we followed, but thick and undisturbed on either side. There were echoes in that big place ... it was curious, the dust muffled like snow, but there were still echoes from the remote darkness ... from far beyond the small spheres of our brief torches in that ancient distance.

"Few have been so far in our confidence and secret places." Craghead turned to leer at me. "We favour you ... favour you all," he turned to include the others. "We favour you, Ice Lover, and look to you for gratitude and servility." He gripped my arm, glanced about and whispered. "Support us against our enemies in our own court!"

"Lord ... we cherish your favour!" we chorused. I was getting to know the game now, it was automatic.

Craghead led on and on. He could sure talk. It was the one thing he could do really well – or you thought so until you listened to what he was saying. He basked in the reflected glory of the old days. He swelled up with the importance of the things he had – the equipment he had hoarded. He was hooked on the stuff – the sense of the power that was there.

I suppose he knew the danger and it was partly that too – the bravado of living in that big bomb. It would have made him real to himself. I don't know what he *thought* it did for him. But there sure was a lot of explosives ... an awesome prospect for some sweet, explosive day.

But what really stopped me was the thing hanging above us in that great barren space. We were walking on in that limited bubble of torchlight same as before –

not seeing much of the place, just conscious of, op-
pressed by, the dark vastness all around, when suddenly
we came to this thing hanging down in front of us. Like
a fly's leg it was. I nearly walked into it.

Giant – all fuzzy with accumulated dust – really big . . .
revolting. I backed off in a hurry and Craghead laughed
at me. He signed one of the guard to hold up a torch so
I could see.

I didn't say anything. I put my pistol away and looked
up at what was above me. It took a while to decide what
it was.

Like a great black moth . . . not quite black . . . *dark* –
yet somehow shining dull metal. Underneath there were
trapdoors hanging open . . . shreds dripped from them –
tubes of rubbery stuff, wires and things like that.

That fly-leg thing came down from one of the traps
in a cascade of looping cables . . . lanky it was . . . *lanky*
and jointed. Made of tubes and more tubes . . . struts
and cross braces. There were four wheels on the end,
all hung and looped with shredded rotten rubber stuff,
hooped and coiled wires mingled with it.

On the underside, when the guard waved his torch
that way, I saw the twin symbol of man – the red and
white stars linked on the oval indigo background, surrounded with that yellow line they say stood for the
sun. I'd never seen one preserved perfect like that before.

It was an aeroplane Craghead said. Made before the
Defeat. Those moth wings came sweeping down, perhaps it was sagging with age. The whole thing was
mounted on some iron trolley thing – the wheels half
sunk in the dust, some sort of test stand I guess – there
was a big panel of dials there and more cables connect-
ing to the belly of the machine.

We walked past another set of those wheeled legs,
then more of the aeroplanes. There may have been a
dozen there forever in that big darkness, I couldn't say,
there could have been hundreds . . . all there hanging like
to dry, to preserve in the smoke like bacon. One thing
was sure, nothing could save them when the place blew

up – nothing would save Craghead either. I had to get to Rutherford. Craghead kept laughing about how that first leg had scared me.

"Well, what do you think?" he said. "How do you like our glories?" There was a murmur of admiration. Craghead grinned, he liked that.

"Lord," said the girl, "tell us how one man can have such things. How can one man be so potent?"

"By hard work and intelligence. A lifetime's long effort. Some of these things were here when first our ancestors led our people Underground to strategically defeat the savage Alien ... but mostly our dynasty has worked out and collected, bought by purchase and conquest, by cunning and politics, the old explosives and strengths. We have all this now – it is our glory and our attributes." I was wondering how they had got those aeroplanes in and how long Craghead had to enjoy his things. If one of those bombs took it into its head to explode – and if it was too near the rest – if just one thing went wrong . . . there'd be no mercy.

"There is more," said Craghead. We moved into an end of the open space. We moved along a blank wall there, through a door maybe nine feet square and into a dim corridor. You could see all four sides in the torch-light and that made me feel a whole lot safer.

At the end there were big doors. Craghead had his grunting, sweating guards thrust them back, then light our way on with their smokey torches.

It was another such place as the hall of the fire. It was lit with a great aisle of pure white candles. Six or seven feet high some of them, maybe they were four inches thick. Some were new and others had burned right down. Men moved amongst them trimming them and replacing those that were finished.

There were guys at the other end, there were piles of gold too, duned, loose on the floor, some on great dishes, all mixed up with loose ammunition like Craghead had given us. There were draperies too – and pictures of the old weapons on the wall behind us. There were more of the big old rockets too – just on the edge of the light – standing on end in their cradles, forming a sort of outer aisle.

When we'd gone maybe fifty yards up the aisle we could see more clearly what the guys there were doing. They had helmets like Craghead's and leaned on reversed rifles, their heads down. They didn't move. Behind them, lying dusty on the floor, were three canvas-and-plastic-wrapped shapes ... very still and bulky. There were some more guys who were kneeling, hands in front of their faces – praying, I suppose.

"Very powerful," said Craghead. "The ultimate thing ... too holy to look directly upon. Three of them I've got. Thermonuclear ... as old as the hills. The most potent thing on earth. Nobody ever made anything better. As long as men pray their virtue will last and be potent. It is a wonderful thing ... the power of prayer."

It was awful ... awesome. Those things, all that power ... all shrouded up – preserved in sanctity – an ark and covenant of power promised for us all down history. I don't know if they were any good after all that time ... I mean, do you really think prayer works? But they certainly were impressive – a noble jewel in Craghead's diadem.

Past those hidden things there was another door. Craghead led us that way and the guards opened that one too. That door was about two feet thick and most of it was lead. There was another exactly the same at the end of a short passage. While they struggled to slide the thing aside I was wondering just what it was that could be beyond those warheads. I mean, what could be deeper? What could need all that lead? I went in, I peered over Craghead, trying to see beyond him

It was books. The place was full of books and tapes. There were long banks of cabinets ... massed steel shelves ... long and dark and green. Loose papers piled about the place, some fixed with rusted staples ... there were broken and disintegrating books ... loose coiled, tangled tapes ... watermarked films, piles of flat, round cans ... bird's nests of wires ... dusty, mysterious in-

77

struments to read them with. Everything must have been written there.

Some of it was on shelves, neat and tidy, but mostly it was scattered on the floor in great loose piles. Man – it was a *mess!*

All the walls were lead-lined – except in one place there was thick double glass and like long gloves reached in in pairs – so that you could do things without actually touching the books, I suppose. There were heavy shutters to cover that glass too. Old Rutherford always used to say they were very dangerous.

"Our books," said Craghead. There were a couple of men in there too. Not old ... not young either ... as hairless as Craghead himself. All covered in sores, skins cracked and appearing to decay ... a lumpy quality about them. One guy had an eye that was white like milk ... his other was red-rimmed and bloodshot, mucus running and crusting on its inside corner. The other man was doubled up, like shrivelled – you could tell he was in pain. After he'd taken a look at us he turned and went away. Craghead didn't seem to mind, he seemed to think something was funny.

The first man came forward and swayed there, looked at us with his one good eye ... as if he was trying to see who we were.

"Our books," said Craghead again. He jerked his thumb at the man. "Our librarian. See what reading does to you. Books are no good to anyone. Learning's a waste of time and does you no good. Ain't no one can tell if you know anything. Don't pay any attention to books!" He thought it was funny. He was laughing. "That librarian – he can read. Look what it's done to him!"

"Lord," the librarian managed at last. "You have things here more potent than your explosives. Things for the future ... a rich treasury.... Let us teach children ..." It was no good, Craghead kept on laughing at him. I guess that guy was – at one time – brighter than Craghead and maybe Craghead knew it and that was why he liked to see him brought down like that.

"Perhaps one day we will know enough to make all the old things work again . . . work – it only needs work . . ."

"Can you do it?" said the girl. "Can you make even a worn-out light work? Can you make our Lord Craghead fly even?" She gestured at that ruined grav unit across Craghead's shoulders. "No! You cannot! Why do they waste their time with books in an attempt to gather the crumbs of yesterday? Make them cease this folly, my Lord Craghead!" I couldn't figure her. I thought she at least would see the value.

"Enough!" said Craghead. "We are tired of this place!"

The librarian turned to me. There was a tear on his cheek, or maybe it was that mucus in the torchlight.

"One day," he said, "one day . . . all knowledge is here . . . promise from the past for our future . . . a way to beat the Aliens. And I am dying for it. . . ." Maybe the girl didn't want to beat the Aliens? But I told myself that was nonsense "Dying . . . for progress. To order this chaos . . . it progresses . . ."

He was right. It was hope – and he was dying for it I could see what he meant . . . but right then I wasn't looking at him and I wasn't listening either. Someone else had just come out from the filing cabinets at the other end of the room. It was Rutherford.

I didn't think he recognized me at first. When I began to speak he frowned and shook his head, so I shut up. I understood afterwards, Craghead's Underground was like that. You didn't reveal anything – you kept as many secrets as you could. It was safer and it got to be automatic.

"The librarian is right, Lord," said Rutherford. "Our best hope for the future is in the books and tapes. They store thought and information . . . power!"

"Pah!" said the girl. "Lord, you have said yourself what knowledge has done for these men! And as for this man's things . . . his crude steam power . . .!" She really hated Old Rutherford. You should have seen her sneer!

"But we must work on, Lord," pleaded Rutherford.

79

"There is much to be done for your greater glory. Soon we may make the wires talk . . ." I saw the girl frown at that. She opened her mouth to speak but Craghead cut her off with a gesture.

"Get you back to your pumps as we have ordered! We will allow the librarian to continue to ruin himself with books . . . these dirty things. He is our tool and expendable. You have your own purpose. Get you to your pumps and make them less . . . less *crude!*" Old Rutherford knew better than to argue with that

Craghead led us out of the chaotic library, through the candle aisle and into the dark spaces. We straggled behind. We said nothing, Craghead talked all the way.

"Guns," he said. "Weapons and *power* . . . being in *charge* . . . the *head* – everything comes second to that . . ." I hurried a little to catch Rutherford. "Power and wealth . . . many servants . . . big guns and many trucks – not paper things – not flimsy tapes . . . Fools!"

It was like that all the way back to the big hall and the activity there. It was very noisy in the hall after the darknesses.

"They are!" said Rutherford suddenly. "Books and knowledge are infinitely valuable. Knowledge is everything there is! We must have the old things or we'll never climb again! How else can we be free?" The fierceness in his voice startled me. He'd been bottling that up all the way back. Then he saw the girl coming across to us so he stopped talking.

"Don't listen to him, Ice Lover," said the girl. "Don't take that romantic drivel too seriously! Knowledge and education indeed! We had that last time and they still beat us. Remember the Defeat! We've got to fight with the weapons we understand – it's practical . . . the only chance of success!" Rutherford grunted and whispered that he'd see me at the engines.

Craghead called me over as soon as he'd regained his dais.

"Ice Lover," he said, "you have seen our power – will you serve us?"

I wondered if I had a choice. Anyway, Craghead sure

had armament, he had an organization – Rutherford was there – what could I do? I nodded. I said yes.

"Then we will find proper use for your talents, Ice Lover. There is much to do." Craghead turned to chatter to his henchmen. I'd been dismissed. I was forgotten again.

I moved off to find Rutherford. I was getting sad once more. Reaction I guess. Or else the state that librarian was in ... that'll come to us all in the end. All Mods anyway ... Free Men too for all I know. Old Rutherford was looking good though – he must have been twice the age most Mods died at. The whole trip too, that depressed me now that I'd actually got that far. It was a long way to come to call a guy "sir" and "worthwhile magnanimous"!

All those deaths and chances of death to bring me here for almost nothing – just to meaningless danger in Craghead's Underground. I suppose in a sort of way it was worth it for Craghead. I was the man that burned the helicopter, everyone seemed to have heard of that. Craghead liked to have famous people round him, he fed on it. It'd be OK for me until he got jealous, a guy had to be careful not to be too good.

I headed off to where the pumps were. Old Rutherford would cheer me up. The girl saw me go, but she was tangled up with Craghead, she had to watch me go.

I was watching things myself right then. The whole air of the place was filled with the drifting sparks – burning bits of rubbish – loose fire floating amongst the smoke and heat. It gave me the horrors.

It was only a question of time before one of those burning bits found one of those sweating bombs. Like fireflies those sparks were ... buzzing about, dangerous up there.

I hurried on. I hoped I'd have time to find Rutherford before the explosion. I bowled through the people – told them they were magnanimous as they sprawled on the floor. I went running as hard as I could into the relative cool of the corridor.

CHAPTER NINE

RUTHERFORD was waiting for me in the shadows a few yards up the corridor.

It was great to talk to the old guy again. Great to talk to another Free Man after all the others. I'd had enough right then. I mean, I wasn't going to stay in that place and be Craghead's dog. I started to say so, but there were people about so Rutherford shut me up. I started to wonder what he was doing there, in that dangerous hot hell of Craghead's. I asked him that and what I should do.

"Wait, son, wait. Don't talk about it. They're like everyone else – they don't like Free Men. Don't say anything where people might hear you." There was so much I wanted to say, to ask him. It was an effort to be quiet.

I showed him the ammunition Craghead had given me. He said – loudly – that it was a fine thing and a mark of great honour, then – softly – how worthless it was. We went on up the corridor.

"I knew it'd be you," he said when we were safe amongst the pumps. "You had to be Ice Lover. You're the only one stupid enough to take on the Aliens like that."

"I'm going to talk to you," I said. "I'm going to talk to you and then I'm going to beat it back to the Tundra. How can you take it? What keeps you here?"

"Ah ... well ... there are things to do. Don't you be a fool! Don't run for it. Craghead would never forgive anyone who tried to get out. What chance would you have in the woods with Craghead's price on your head?"

"What things to do? You know about those explosives? Well – they're dangerous .. the place is stuffed with 'em! So why? Why do you stay?"

"Well ... there are questions." He paused to check that there was no one about. "Like why Free Men exist at all after twelve generations of mixing. How many are there ... who is and who isn't? Like who are the Aliens ... those you got up on the Tundra ... were they really Aliens – or some sort of Superwardens? They don't seem like the description you find in the legends ... the old wives don't talk about them being like that! Like what's on the level beneath this one ... and that girl – how does she stay celibate? What's her axe she's grinding here?"

"I can tell you some of that," I said. "Drugs stop her being a Breeder – she told me." Then I filled Rutherford in on how she'd saved me in that inn – brought me to Craghead. He wondered what she saw in me and I asked him what this was about a lower level.

"Yes ... the pumps, that's my best reason for being here." He was looking at me very hard under those brows of his, I started to wonder where the girl got her antilove pills – which is what Rutherford meant by looking at me like that. From the ice I suppose ... where everybody got everything.

"I've got it working really well now." Rutherford started showing me round his pumps. That girl was getting to be a mystery – I'd have to watch her. "Very simple of course ... atmospheric. You fill a cylinder with steam, cool it and the pressure drop inside lets the atmosphere shove on the piston and gives you the power stroke. Easy to make even with the materials and tools we've got – no high-pressure steam to blow you up ... there were some better engines in the book, this was earliest and best for our purpose – you can plug leaks with a handful of clay. I transmit the energy to the pumps with that rocker!" He meant the seesaw arrangement across the top. We stood there and admired the slow power of the thing. I congratulated him.

"Not *efficient*," he said. "You lose so much when you cool it. It works though. I've got ten of them in various parts of the Underground ... dropping the water nearly two feet a day – unless it rains ..."

"Lower level?" He's a great man, but he forgets sometimes.

"Ah ... I'm pumping it out. Find out what's there. Below this ... down there under the water .. down the shaft. Craghead thinks there'll be munitions there ... so he gives me the gear and the men. Maybe there will be .. I hope so ... but it's curiosity really ... I'd like to know. It must have flooded pretty quickly after the Defeat ... maybe even before ... things'll be pretty much as they were ... I'll learn a lot. It could be very important .. the human remains should be very interesting."

"Suppose this place blows in the meantime?"

"Do you know I believe I've stopped caring ... worrying anyway? I reckon another week or two – maybe less – to dry the lower level. It's been a long job ... when we've finished and we've found what there is to find I'll be happy. It's curiosity that keeps a man going."

"OK – so I'll risk it – so I'll hang about for a while. There's not much here for me though. Can I work with you–"

"No," Rutherford was incisive now, he'd snapped out of his philosophical dreams. "You go to Craghead and listen. See what you can find out ... especially about that girl." He went and did something to the nearest engine. "Yes ... stay close to the girl ... find out what she's up to."

I said good-bye and went back to the hall. All right – so I'd stay. I didn't have to like it ... I could be plenty scared if I wanted. It was good to see Rutherford again. Good to know someone was still doing something.

So I was hanging about the Underground, in that hot and dangerous hall for what seemed like weeks. It was a plain bore most of the time. I got in the odd fight, but they were all so scared of my pistol that it was painful they were so polite to me.

Once in a while I went to talk and report to Rutherford but he was busy with his pumping. They'd got a hundred or so feet pumped out but it was getting slower and slower. The pumps were near their limit and the rubbish down there kept clogging the pickups and they had to haul them up all the time to clear them.

All sorts of things they took out of those pipes. Sheets of metal, tools, bodies – all the junk that had been thrown down from Craghead's level, things like that ... bones and rotting flesh ... great lumps of blue-green rotting slush.

Rutherford made baskets to put on the pickups and then it wasn't too bad. When a basket clogged they let some water run back and that cured it.

Then he had himself lowered in a bucket on a rope off the treadmill. He went down into darkness with a torch in each hand – red sparks and light disappearing down the wet shaft, that soupy water glinting and stinking below. They managed to dunk him in the stuff but he came up shouting with excitement and not anger like I thought at first.

There were battle signs down there, he said. He'd seen bullet scars and burned places from explosions and fires. The water was still above the roof of any corridors that might be down there, but he was more convinced than ever that there was something down there ... some palace from before the Defeat.

Then it rained and the water rose again – every time it rained the water came up several feet now. So Craghead found more men and materials and Rutherford began to build more pumps further down the shaft. With the news of the bullet marks Craghead got really interested and the work went on real fast.

The girl didn't have a lot to say either. When I asked her what was happening and what I was to be used for she'd only say that plans were being made and supplies collected. I said I was pretty fed up and had almost decided to make it back to the Tundra. Not that it was much more than a thought by then – I was only trying to provoke her to say something.

"Don't be a fool," she said. "How do you think you'd even get through the guards? What do you think it'd be like in the woods with all them after you? I can't protect you if you try and leave." It was uncanny – it was exactly like talking to Rutherford.

"The only thing that keeps me here is Old Rutherford – I mean that guy that's pumping . . . what he may find down there." I'd nearly said too much.

"Rutherford? That madman on the pumps? You know him?"

"Hell yes! Now let go of my arm – I'm not going any place!" What did I care what a Breeder knew or thought she knew? She was right though – I wouldn't get ten miles in the woods.

"So you know Rutherford? A friend?" She looked at me thoughtfully. "From the ice, I suppose?"

"Yeah."

"Know anything about him? Where he comes from – what he wants . . . what his modifications are?" Trust a Breeder to ask questions like that. You just don't ask what a man's modifications are – it's not decent.

"No." Rutherford had told me to be careful of her.

"You watch him. Be careful – mind what you say . . . he's mysterious. Sometimes I suspect . . ." She looked at me hard, weighing what she was going to say. "Sometimes I think he might be a Free Man!"

"What – are there any of them left?" I could be clever too. "You ought to be careful . . . he's close to Craghead!" We looked around and felt furtive . . . she knew very well you shouldn't talk like that.

"Some . . . somewhere," she murmured. She seemed to lose interest then. "Don't wander off . . . stay where I can find you – it won't be long now. And stop starting fights."

Man – but they were zombies! Those Mods walking that Underground. You couldn't provoke them! All they thought about was their positions in Craghead's court, not getting in bad with him, not demeaning themselves by actually doing anything. Walking slowly – then jumping with enthusiasm when he spoke. It was a pretty dull time.

I used to go a lot and listen to that musician. He'd play and sing for anyone who'd listen . . . I saw the girl there a lot. There'd be tears in her eyes and then maybe she'd have a long talk with the guy. The kids used to listen to him too.

I remember one of the songs. Partly that is, it didn't rhyme or anything. It was the music that tied it up, I'd hum it for you if I could. It stuck in my mind because it made me think of the Tundra, about snowflakes. I guess maybe it was really about the Defeat:

Slow drift down . . . Falling ending . . .
All individual all different . . . also similar . . .
Or so they say . . . All die, go away . . .
Slow drift down . . . Or up, in space it doesn't mat-
   ter . . .
All in the long accumulation of time . . .
All ending in the long passage of time . . .

It was curious because the order it came in didn't matter either – that all depended on the music – and you remembered it the way you had to. I guess it meant different things for different people. It was very sad, but there was a hope in it too – about the snow ending I mean – if that was what it was about. But everybody who listened knew that guy was telling you *something*.

Then Craghead sent for me. I left off kicking my heels and went and sweated in front of that dais again. The girl was there too, up behind him, stooping, whispering.

"Ice Lover," said Craghead when he had stopped pretending not to see me, "we have a task . . . a *mission* for you!" "Mission" was the word that week. You know: "mission for life", "man's mission", stuff like that.

"You accept, Ice Lover?" said the girl. She nodded frantically. She was behind Craghead and he couldn't see her. I would have liked to know exactly what I was letting myself in for, but I looked at the girl signalling there and accepted. Hell – you've got to trust people – sometimes, I mean – and this job might take me outside. Who *was* that girl anyway – she kept helping me and I couldn't figure it.

"Approach us," said Craghead. "This mission is secret, privy to us and not for common ears!"

87

I climbed up onto the dais and stood beside him. You could see right out over the people – over the variegated heads all masked in smoke, receding to obscurity and darkness. Then there was that fire roaring and swirling into its cowl ... all those fiery sparks sailing and drifting about the place. I made an effort and stopped thinking about the bombs.

"Sit beside us," said Craghead. There was no seat, he meant the floor – it was pretty hard there. That old hairless head leered down at me. His skin had a lilac cast about it that day. That's a thing about Mods – how they seem to vary from day to day.

"Thank you, Lord." I was really curious to find out about what he had in mind for me. I might even get a chance to escape.

"It's south. It's a mission south, Ice Lover!" He watched the effect of that on me. It was like a mule kick in the heart. "We would send you south into and through the Border. In quest of the foul Alien. To scout for us, to test defences ... the readiness of the Wardens ... perhaps even to get sight of the Aliens themselves." He broke off and shook with giggles. "What, Ice Lover – scared? *You* scared? Are you frightened that your rabbit whiskers tremble so?" For a guy that lived in a hole he was sure fond of calling people rabbits.

"No, Lord," I said when I'd controlled my face. I mean – *south!* No man had set foot there – except as a slave – since before the Defeat! Beyond the dead places ...! Sure I was scared. So would you have been. It was a sentence of death or horror worse than death.

"I will go," I said as calmly as I could. "It will be interesting. Those are mysterious areas." Bloody-minded old fool! The thought came that this might be his way of getting rid of me ... maybe I was too good for him.

"We will send companions with you. Our good girl ... armed Riders. Remember you are in Craghead's employ – uphold our honour in far places. Our good girl will arrange all details."

And that was all. Craghead started to play with that

88

skull in a carapace that he had. Up close I could see he was decorating it, carving and engraving patterns on the horny outside. Well – it was a hobby I suppose.

The girl led me down off the dais and we went out through the milling and purposeless crowd. We went down the main corridor, Rutherford wasn't at his engines and I didn't dare leave any message. In a place like Craghead's with all that concentration of Mods there were bound to be some spies. I'd just have to tell him about it when we got back ... or not at all if we didn't.

Under the treadmill the water was well down – out of sight now. It looked like the pumps were winning after all. There was a new engine about every fifty feet down the shaft – it was murderously hot for the poor devils on the treadmill. I thought I saw Rutherford down there, but I didn't get a chance to speak to him. The girl was in a hurry.

When we reached the surface we had to rest under some trees for quite a while, it was blinding up there after so long underground. It was good to get in fresh air though. You don't realize how a place stinks until you get out of it.

When we were ready that old blue truck was there waiting for us. There were two or three horsemen as well. They didn't like leaving their horses, but the girl spoke to them and convinced them the Border was no place to go horseback riding.

We all piled in and the girl drove us off. Those guys were maybe the most modified I'd seen in Craghead's Riders. The girl said she'd chosen them so they wouldn't be too obvious further south.

Even the village looked good, it was nice to see kids again – even if they were Mods. I was glad to be on the surface, out of those explosives. Just for a moment it seemed that the world was a lot to lose after all, a lot to go south from.

We passed out through the canyon walls and the gates there. There were trees growing up there – sycamores mostly, the leaves looked great with the sun shining through them. There was more water there, all running out that way from Rutherford's pumps.

We drove across that short road and turned west. We'd almost reached the beech woods when there was a shout and we saw young Craghead waiting for us in the shade.

"It is a great adventure," he said. "I cannot be left behind." It was that simple for him.

The girl looked at him. He sat still on his great horse, but you could see the tension on the guy's face. He really wanted to go. Fool. At first I thought she would refuse but she relented and nodded.

He turned his horse loose to find its own way home, climbed into the truck and sat between the girl and me on the front bench. He was quiet for a while but he soon started talking again, happy as a kid on an outing.

We went west along the wood's edge and when we were out of sight of the Enclosure we turned south for the Border. The air was warm, there was just the slightest breeze, a sweet smell in the air and I got hay fever. Young Craghead started to get on my nerves, so I went to sleep. I was tired, I hadn't slept too well in the Underground.

I woke and we were carefully picking our way through the last unhealthy trees before the Border. Heat shimmered out there, the blue-black eroded hills faded into wavering distance. It was like a glimpse of hell. I wondered if there was any way I could dodge this trip. It was all wrong. There were too many of us for a start – one man might make it – not a truckload. Come to that no one ought to go, it was too dangerous.

We hid up there in those last trees and waited for darkness. I played dice with the Riders while we waited that long afternoon away. The girl sat to one side, on a stump, you could tell she had a worried mind. She was right – you'd have been worried too.

Mists came with evening. White vapours which filled the valleys first, then rose up to mask the higher ground. When that happened we moved. One of the Riders who had infra-red sat up front and told the girl where to drive. I don't know why we waited, the Aliens – and some Wardens – can see in the dark too, it was daft, but we felt safer.

It was uncanny. The way that truck slithered on on its cushion, uphill and down again, the motors humming as we went sliding and scuffing through the fog, through and around the broken things in that landscape, stuff we couldn't see.

We came out once. On a hill. We went skimming up and up that slope and – just for a second we were in clear air.

It was fantastic. Just for a flash there we were on that hummock surrounded with starlit ocean. There were one or two dark headlands and you could see bits of ruins and girders sticking up. Then we were in fog again. The night was more than half gone and there was no sign of an end. Young Craghead was asleep. He sure snored loud. The girl looked worried, like I say the night was more than half gone – it was getting *late*. I hoped Craghead's snoring wouldn't wake anything better left asleep.

Then the girl said we'd not make the south that night, that we ought to be under cover by dawn. Hell, I thought, they were probably watching us all the way in some subtle machine they probably had. Then the guy who was seeing for us said there was a ruin up ahead and maybe we should hide there.

It was just another of those old farm places. Standing steel and concrete, a few tatters of plastic, nothing had lived there for ages. In the morning I saw a couple of those old silo things, all leaning they were ... cracking up too.

We drove the truck into roofless walls and as the fog lightened with the dawn, scattered it with stones and mud to hide it some. When the girl cut the motors we listened really hard, but there was nothing.

91

CHAPTER TEN

WHEN the sun came up and the fog was disappearing the girl and I went and looked south through where there had been a window.

It was a hard way we had to go. The first three or four miles were the same black, broken ground. Then that stopped and when the mist there was gone you could see it was flat. Like a pancake ... like one of those floors in the Underground. We couldn't see much of what was beyond that – it was too far – but it looked like the Border ran right on to the horizon. There were what looked like mountains flashing white with snow over cloud, but they could have been twenty or several hundred miles off. It was all lost in haze and distance, you couldn't really tell.

The girl had a pair of field glasses, she was making a real study of things. I stood beside her and wished she'd give me a turn with them. She did in the end, when I asked her.

That flat plain ... it was made of iron – or something like it. Where it was eroded you could see the joins in it ... seams and joining edges. I remarked on it, but the girl didn't make anything of it.

"Have you looked at those mountains?" she said.

They were something too. All regular ... angled structures ... lights flashed off them. Where the sun hit them you were almost blinded. Like glass – much brighter than what I'd thought was snow. Buildings? A city. It dawned on me it was a city!

"My God!"

'Yes," said the girl. "Artifact ... architecture – it must be enormous ..." She wouldn't speculate though, all she'd say was: "Wait and see."

The girl said she'd keep watching and I went back to

where a dice game was starting and sent one of the
Riders up to watch from the ridge. Then I settled down
to a morning's sport.

"Well?" said young Craghead when he couldn't contain himself any longer. "What's there, Ice Lover?"

"Country ... bare, dead country. All filled with am-
bushing deadly Aliens."

"What?" It took him a moment to see I was kidding.
That's something else about Mods – they don't have
much sense of humour. Anyway, I pretended to go to
sleep after we'd eaten and pretty soon I really did. I
surely couldn't face Craghead for all day.

I woke to crashing shots. I struggled up to the window
and saw maybe ten or a dozen Wardens closing in on
us.

Craghead's boys were on the ridge and they'd fired
too soon. The Wardens hadn't even bothered to take
cover. You could see bullets thumping dust out of the
body armour – sometimes kicking lumps out of a carapace here and there. Once in a while a Warden would
get knocked down – but that's all it was, they were soon
up again. The bullets weren't penetrating.

I fired a couple of times and hit one. He didn't get
up again – he was bleeding all over the place. They took
cover when they saw what my pistol could do. It was
no good though. You could see what was going to happen.

I crouched along the wall to a doorway where young
Craghead and the girl were. She was telling him how he
should have kept his men under better control. She told
me how I shouldn't have gone to sleep. She was white
with rage.

"Cut the row!" I said. "We've got to get out. They'll
fry us!"

"Yeah," said Craghead. "Yeah."

I looked again and the Wardens had stopped. One
was carefully aiming with that tube weapon they have.
The rest were waiting while he got his shot.

I didn't hesitate. I dived back down the slope towards

the building where the truck was. The rest came tumbling after.

Hellfire danced all along the ridge crest. I swear I got burned with a spot of molten brick from the wall. There was a dull thud and a sort of explosion as the soil dried and cracked up. A dust cloud leapt up and drifted downwind towards the Wardens.

One of the Riders came staggering and falling down to us about then. He'd been caught and he was dead really ... half of him was about burned away. Still – he'd watched plenty of people die in front of that fire in the Underground. You couldn't really shed any tears for him.

We got up out of the rubble and spat out the scalding dust. We took a look at each other and ran for the truck.

The girl started the motor and we moved out camouflage and all. I did a quick count. Young Craghead was there – the girl, me – of course – and a couple of Riders.

"Hit it!" I yelped. "Go like hell!" The girl banged the throttles open and we shot off west along the ridge.

"Up the hill!" I screamed. "Into the dust cloud – charge them!" It was what they wouldn't expect.

She nodded. She spun the control. The truck went slithering and screaming up the slope. I was scared. I mean *really* scared.

The Wardens had sure churned up that ridge. To our left they were still doing it. The whole summit was alive with fire and explosions. A running stream of dust blew south across the Wardens. The came forward in it like automatons, still firing at where they'd last seen us.

The girl drove south through the dust by compass. We didn't think to use the Mod with infra-red in that stuff – I guess maybe it was that Rider who got killed. I stood up with my pistol and looked forward over the windshield. Young Craghead was there too.

We saw a couple of Wardens close to. One was straight in front and the girl ran him down. He was standing so there was a heck of a bump and I thought for a moment we'd turn over. I took a shot at him as he came out the back but we were going too fast. It all added to the dust. Then there was the one young Crag-head got. Right in the face. A beautiful shot – made him happy all day.

Suddenly we were out. Still driving and bucking south, going fast out onto the iron plain. I say iron – but you couldn't be sure – we were going too fast and we surely weren't going to stop to look.

It was surprising. It was only another thirty miles and we made it easy. A quarter of an hour and then we were in the first foothills, then through them and into the start of vegetation again. All that time the Wardens couldn't see us for the dust cloud. As far as I could see they were still burning away the top of the ridge.

"Did anyone see if those last Wardens had communicator eyes?" said the girl.

No one knew for sure, but we thought not. If that was right then there was a chance the Aliens hadn't seen which way we went. Maybe they'd think we were dead and it might be OK.

Pretty soon after that we were well hidden in plants. They weren't all Alien, but a lot were. I tried to look up and see that city thing ahead, but that was out of sight beyond the foothills and vegetation.

Threading through those trees and Alien stuff it slowly dawned on us we'd made it. We were there! We'd made it into the south.

There didn't seem to be anyone trying to kill us right then, for the moment we were as safe as we'd ever be. We grinned at each other as we bucketed along – it was like being drunk – we didn't care. Man – we'd made it! Across the *Border!* We'd *made* it! Now we'd start to find out!

We just forgot time. Quite suddenly it was dusk and there were lights in a valley to the left.

We remembered where we were then – it brought us up short. God knew what dangers there were down there. The girl cut the motors and we slithered quietly into undergrowth on the last power of the fans We were quiet then, sitting in the gloom, staring down at those dangerous lights. It started to rain and we stayed there all night.

In the morning it was still raining but we left the truck anyway and scouted about some. Down where we'd seen the lights there was a small sodden huddle of buildings. We went down very cautiously.

There was nothing mysterious about it – we've all seen a thousand like it. As the dawn fought through the sagging nimbus and the birds began a half-hearted chorus for it, we watched from wet bushes and cursed our soaking feet. Then the Riders started to look mutinous so we moved into the mud street.

We found an inn amongst the houses – just like any other. We were getting braver as we got wetter – and it all seemed so ordinary – so we went in. It was just exactly what you'd expect in there – we might just as well have never left home. We bought some booze and that was just exactly the same too. It was a bit of an anti-climax.

It seemed OK so we mingled with the people there and asked a few questions. We couldn't get anyone to really open up though. They didn't trust us, they wouldn't say anything about further south and they were just as frightened of questions about the north. You know – there are some things you don't talk about . . . it was the same here. It was like home.

Then young Craghead asked something directly about the Aliens and all the people stared at us and then most of them left. We finished our drinks and got out of there. Some spy or other followed us but young Craghead waited and hit him over the ear with a gun butt. We left the guy lying in the mud and got away like that.

We made it about five miles south then hit a clump of heavy Alien stuff. It didn't look very inviting. Sullen . . . close-grown wiry stuff that shivered and flexed . . . like contracted then expanded again. It was quite shallow at first but about fifty yards in it went straight up.

Like a wave it was a great breaker, frozen when it was at its highest. I'd seen waves like that up on the Tundra. It stretched east and west forever, it was much bigger than I'd thought at first. Anyway, we reckoned there might be Wardens after us by then so we started heading into it.

As a matter of fact the going wasn't too bad. That stuff pushed aside quite easily when you shoved, it was half soft and half sticky too. When you looked behind you could see the fibres moving back behind you. Not springing – *moving*. It was funny, but you could wriggle and push through it all right. We had to leave the truck. It just took time to penetrate, that's all. We tried to keep our feet on the ground and went on.

Quite suddenly there were clear pockets in the stuff, they got bigger and soon after that we were out under the sky again.

The air was dry and warm ... clean on your face. We were in a flowery meadow ... in sunlight, looking across regular agricultural acres towards those bright mountain-buildings heaving up above the far horizon. We seemed to have come a long way pretty quickly. There were strange things like that all the time we were in the Aliens' country ... something about time and distance there, it was so *subjective*. There were earth plants there, trees ... brambles and nettles ... it was *good* to be out ... the flowers smelled good too.

I wasn't sure if those mountains were artificial or not. Sometimes I thought they were – then a minute later I was sure they weren't ... they were pretty regular though. It wasn't so much that they were so far away – but the sun was on them and dazzled you. They were further away the more I looked at them ... maybe we hadn't come so far after all ... you couldn't tell. They were beautiful .. like diamonds in the sky ... like I say, it was a confusing sort of place.

There was someone waiting for us. A guy in a truck. A Mod ... he had four arms – he kept the delicate ones curled up against his chest like a squirrel when he wasn't using them ... he had what looked like a flower in his hair . . . he wasn't armed – but what really surprised me was he looked so proud.

I stood very still and looked at him. He was grinning all over his face. He stood upright, he was clean . . . he was noble and cheerful . . . there was something very odd about him. The girl and the rest of them came straggling out of the thicket and shambled up beside me.

Craghead swore and started to drag out his gun. The guy on the truck lost his smile and stepped out the other side. He got the body of the truck between us and him and I held Craghead's gun down.

"No," I said. "There's only one . . . wait!" This guy was different. He was happy for one thing. I wanted to know why. There was plenty of time to shoot him if we had to. The girl said something short and forceful to Craghead and he stopped struggling.

"Thank you," said the Mod behind the truck. "I am Cristan – I am your guide . . . you have nothing to fear from me. Welcome, I am a friend." I felt dirty – like a savage.

We looked at each other a while longer then that Cristan guy said to come down and he'd take us where we wanted to go. The girl asked how he knew enough to meet us. He smiled and said that he knew and that we'd been watched.

Well – we did it! Walked down like he said. I was almost surprised to find myself in that truck when I thought about it. I mean, trusting the guy like that! We were lulled by him . . . he was so *charming* – you just *knew* he wouldn't clobber you.

It was the countryside too. It was beautiful . . . relaxed into blue-heat distance – so different from all those unkempt beech woods . . . the battle ruins snarled there. Anyway, we had guns and Cristan didn't.

"I will take you south," he said. "South to our town there, our home." Still south . . . I seemed fated that way, further and further from my Tundra. It was different this time though. I didn't feel so worried about it . . . it looked so pleasant and warm ahead.

Cristan drove off. The truck was just the same as the

girl's. It was better though, it had cushions and there was still paint on it. There weren't any blades missing from the fans so it ran a lot smoother and sounded different too. You could hear yourself talk without shouting.

We went down through that pleasant meadow, through rushes and tall flowers and onto a road there. It was a nice place, a smiling, happy land.

"What's that place we came through?" said the girl.

"The Thicket," said Cristan, smiling. "It's to protect us from the north." He made a small quick movement with his secondary hands. "I'm sorry ... I mean the troubles they tell us are to the north. ..." Nobody minded, he was a *nice* guy.

"How far does it go?" said Craghead. "Can it be out-flanked?"

"Round the world," said Cristan, as though this was the most natural thing. "We are protected from every direction." He must have known what young Craghead was thinking, but he didn't say anything.

"How long has it been there?" said the girl. "That is, who made ... planted it?"

Cristan shook his head and smiled. The guy didn't know, or he wouldn't tell us – but what did that matter anyway? I didn't mind. Then he said: "But maybe our Fathers will tell you."

"How can a thing like that keep guys out? We came through easy enough," said young Craghead, transparent as ever.

"It varies ... it watches and varies. A man can get through almost always ... sometimes more than one. Sometimes even our people go north ..." He didn't seem too clear about that, maybe he couldn't understand it, or didn't want to talk of it.

"Who made it?" said the girl more quietly than last time.

"That you must ask our Fathers," said Cristan. "See our good fields – the irrigation ... the richness and pleasantness of our land."

It was pleasant too. Rolling away ... relaxing, all lush

and well-kept away into the distance. The way things ought to be ... agricultural – *husbanded*. I put my head on the sun-warm seat back and searched through my furs for my tobacco. Cristan saw what I wanted and gave me one of his cigarettes. He lit it for me with a thing from the dash. The girl's truck didn't have one of those. I folded my arms and closed my eyes. I felt great. It was like coming home. It was easy ... *easy*.

It was a tree-lined road and we went south along it. East and west the fields got lusher and lusher. Those crops – some of it was sugarcane maybe – I couldn't decide ... they were in long parallel clumps running away to the horizon. There were some guys working near the road every few hundred yards, there seemed to be some sort of centre in the irrigation in those places.

Everything ran in deep wooden troughs that started maybe thirty feet above ground then ran slightly down to distribute the fluid. A canal ran beside the road, there were big wheels with buckets on them which tipped into the troughs as they reached the top. The men worked the wheels by standing on the spokes, kind of walking up them. It was like Craghead's treadmill but smoother, I never saw any pumps or anything. I thought about how Rutherford could help them and how I'd have to tell Cristan when I thought about it. I saw no animals working, there were some more of the trucks ... but men did most of the work.

The guys on the wheels waved to us as we passed, Cristan waved back, they were all laughing. We waved too, it was nice. In the distance, to the east and west, you could see more of the wheels.

"It looks like a lot of work," I said.

"It is a happiness. It is good to have things to do ... to work and be fulfilled in labour. To know that you have work to do, to do it, and to know that it is valued. We are happy. This is the Happy Land ..." It looked like a good life ... it sure did ... the flowers were wonderful.

We went south ... speeding south along that good road, towards the warm sun. Nobody said much, it was so relaxing. You could smell the blossom all the way. A heady sort of drowsy summer day Up ahead I noticed that angular glass mountain again. As we went down between those trees it kept flashing at me through the leaves. After a while I asked Cristan what it was.

"Don't you like it?"

"Well . . . yes, I suppose."

"Beautiful . . . beautiful. . . ."

"Well – yes – it's beautiful. It's a building? Your city? What's it made of?"

"Lights and crystals of light. . . . Rainbows and spectrums of beauty. Don't you like crystals?"

"Yes . . . I suppose so. Is it natural then?"

"Beautiful. Useful too."

"It's big. How long is it?" After a moment I asked: "How useful?"

"Yes . . . yes. Gathers light. Reflects it . . . stores it too for colder times . . . nights. Compared to it the Thicket is dead. Light for agriculture. Beautiful too."

"Ah . . ." I was convinced. It was beautiful and that was what mattered. It hurt your eyes but it was the best thing I'd seen in my life. This was a *happy* land – *the* Happy Land. Everything was so beautiful and so rich.

"All around the world. On the equator . . . the place of maximum light . . . it's right. So reasonable . . . so beautiful!"

It was. It *was!* A happy land. *Happy* Land. Everything . . . that word happy . . . it fitted . . . it *fitted!*

"Happy is our land," said Cristan. "In love and faith and work." I felt too good to listen, I didn't even notice what he was saying. I was happy. It was the most natural thing in the world. I puffed my smoke and smiled at the sun.

Somewhere someone was singing quietly to himself. It was young Craghead. It surprised me but I didn't notice. Maybe I was asleep or something. It was beautiful.

CHAPTER ELEVEN

THEN it was a still summer evening and we made it to Cristan's town.

That was beautiful too. Stone houses built in elegant proportions, set in gardens of magnolias and camellias, bright pink flowering bushes, the place filled with scent ... dark bushes, hedging us, cut to intricate, many-patterned topiary. All glowing in the retained light of the Crystal Mountains ... and behind again the million stars that shone that evening.

I stood in the garden and smelled the night blossom. Then the girl was there somewhere. I put my arm round her and she came close. I loved everybody and I loved her ... it was a *softness*. The beauty of that place ... the Happy Land was lovely and there were no tensions or mistrusts. All hate was gone, for the first time I was content ... *really* content I mean.

I'd kissed the girl some when Cristan came and started to pull at my arm.

"Time to go," he said. "Time to eat and to meet our people." For a moment there was a flash of my old anger. I started to draw back my fist to punch him. I, mean, interrupting a guy like that. But he looked so innocent standing there with that soft flower in his hair, so surprised to see my fist up, that I couldn't. You know – a punch wouldn't have fitted then and there. The girl didn't seem to mind at all, they're like that when they're not Breeders.

"You must eat now," said Cristan.

I went first, the girl was a little behind, fixing her dress. It was a high room, well lit and pleasant. The walls were smooth, plastered maybe, painted too ... all in beautiful and loving colours. There was good glass and pottery on the loaded tables. People were sitting there already, none of them were what you'd call heavily modified – nothing I noticed anyway – men and women all together.

Cristan introduced us round, he said we were strangers from the north, come to see the Happy Land. He said we'd expected slavery and oppression here, slavemaster Aliens, that we'd have to fight for our lives. He said it was a wonder how rumour grew, how men, envying what they did not understand, always hated what was better. There was a sad nodding of heads, but people were soon talking again, they were all so *happy*.

Then someone asked me if he could relieve me of my heavy pistol. Now, I've never parted with that. I sure wasn't going to then. I stared at the guy. I mean, part with your *weapon!* What next! I was more puzzled than angry.

"What . . . frowning?" said Cristan at my elbow. He put his arm in mine. "Smile," he said. "Don't waste energy being angry."

I felt the tension flow from me. I suddenly felt how ugly that scowl was on my face. I made an effort and got rid of it. I shivered.

"No, don't ask for his gun. In its way it is a rich thing – a fine thing," said Cristan to the man who had asked for the gun. He turned back to me. "No, Ice Lover . . . you keep it. It's *yours*."

Dirty, noisy, oily . . . guns smelled. I could see that. It struck me just how heavy it was too – fancy carrying a thing like that about all the time. Somewhere, in the back of my head, I started to wonder what he knew about Ice Lover.

"He's an old bore," said the girl. She was all laughing high spirits, all twinkling and bright. "Ignore him, Cristan, he was too long in the ice. Talk to me instead."

"It means nothing here," said Cristan. "All is love and peace. Guns or no guns, it is all the same. Only another useless machine from the old days." He laughed and pushed a flower in my hair. "One of us now . . . all together!" He went off with his arm around the girl and his hand on her hip.

I remember eating. The food looked the same as that stuff they doled out in the north. It tasted different though ... rich like the herrings I used to have sometimes on the Tundra ... or like the beef you found in tins if you were lucky. There was beer to drink too ... at least I suppose it was beer. Anyway, it was a good meal. Then they brought out some spirits and the party really got going. I wondered how I ever thought I liked it up on the Tundra ... up in those sterile, barren places.

There was music and dancing. Some songs and being together. I got a woman later on – not the girl – an ordinary Breeder I thought. I took her out in the garden, but she had the webbed thigh modification so it wasn't very good. She smiled and I didn't mind, I loved her all the same and I felt great. Later, when it had gone quieter, they played different music and someone sang some songs that were really lovely. I was back with the girl by then and we held hands.

When it was all finished they showed us where we were to sleep and we turned in. I slept with the girl, but nothing came of it. In a way it was that I respected her too much. It was a new experience all round. It was marvellous.

I thought how great it would be to go back and convert Old Craghead. Tell all the people in the north how good it was here ... how well Cristan's people ran things. Then I thought no ... that I'd stay there and enjoy it a while first. Maybe there was something wrong though ... maybe it was all a bit too good to be true. I wondered who the "Fathers" were ... and why they needed to run all those tough Wardens if they were so peaceful. Then I thought how they had to protect their success ... protect their very existence. They had to look after themselves ... we couldn't have all those northern barbarians flooding south. It would ruin it all for us.

If Craghead and everybody would only cooperate more amongst themselves and with the Wardens it would be so much better. Everybody would have a Happy Land then ... far, far away up in the Borderlands. Perhaps I could be a prophet ... convert them

104

... create a new situation, make love and sweetness and light. Perhaps there was hope yet.

Somewhere I could hear young Craghead drinking and singing still. That made me think of my gun so I went and got it. Force of habit I suppose.

The gun stank too much under my cheek ... too hard too. So I put it in the crook of my knee which is a pretty good place too. I thought it was strange how I'd only just realised how basically nasty guns are. I was drowsing ... I was warm and comfortable .. the girl was really *soft*.

Somewhere, far away, Craghead stopped singing. Somewhere someone was being sick. That Craghead, he was a beast ... a real low Mod. He was revolting ... how could he fit in here ... two-faced and treacherous. But I loved him too.

The girl now ... she was soft and comfortable. Then I went to sleep.

There was someone bouncing on my stomach and I woke up.

The girl was stooped over me and shaking me by the hair. It was young Craghead doing the bouncing. The girl's blouse was open to her navel and she was sure shaking me.

"Get up! GET UP! Wake! Damn you, WAKE!" She had me up then and I was sitting up in bed wondering what time it was and what it would take to stop Craghead. I managed to kick him off and yelled some.

Craghead landed in a heap on the floor. He sat there in a pool of something that smelled nasty. Vomit it was ... vomit. He was groaning and holding his head. Fool, I thought, trust young Craghead to get sick at a party. I looked at him and felt contemptuous. The place stank. Then the goodwill came flooding back and I forgave everyone. The sick smell faded and all I got was the night perfume from the garden.

I put my arms round the girl and my head on her shoulder. It was soft there. She had an arm round my back and she was holding me up. That was nice too.

"My good, good girl," I said. I loved her and everybody. She was holding a beaker to my mouth.

"Drink," she said. I pushed it back and kissed her neck. She shoved me back and there was the beaker under my nose again.

"Drink," she said. I didn't want a drink. I wanted her. Her fingers clamped on my nose. I drank.

Rare wine. It was beautiful. Then something went wrong. It was salt. All the seas boiled down into a pint mug. *Salt!* Salt as hell.

"Flies' wings!" she said. "Bluebottle pie . . wings between your teeth . . . leg scratch on your gullet!"

I heaved. My stomach contracted. I gagged . . . tried to make it to the window. My only thought was for the rug there. Ochre and red in soft contrasts. Salt as seven seas in one . . . and a dish of flies in my mind's eye . . . a corpse I saw once all dark bluebottles and green corruption underneath.

I made it to the window. It was open. I thought I'd never stop. My belly ached with repeated retchings. It was terrible . . . terrible. Once . . . when I thought I'd finished . . . I looked up there to that Crystal Mountain range . . . lovely and lightful . . . immaculate in its beauty. Then I had to look down and watch my puke splash on the ground . . . I shut my eyes and heard it splatter there. And the girl was always somewhere . . . always close with that damn salt water.

When at last I came away from that window I was a new man. An empty one . . . an old one . . . drained and washed out. I found a chair and sat down. I put my face in my hands and groaned like Craghead. No one moved. Someone was sobbing and it was me.

The girl walked to where there was a ewer. There were washing sounds. I looked up and saw her pale naked back. I looked down again . . . I was too nearly dead to care. Hell – she was a Mod anyway. I felt about in the sticky blankets and found my gun.

"God – what a wet" said young Craghead. "What a party! I've been sick four times!" He seemed proud.

"Drugs," said the girl. "Lotus eaters. Tranquillizers

106

and worse. We're lucky. It was nearly too late." I got up and made it to the ewer. I splashed my face. "They nearly got us," the girl went on. "Those flowers ... the air, the music ... and the food. I've heard of things like that. It's a Happy Land OK. Happy all the time!

"We were lucky ... some people can't take those drugged smokes of Cristan's. Intolerant ... an allergy. Craghead was one. He came to love me ... as he leaned down he threw up ... so I was sick too ... sympathetic. It cured us. Then we got the salt from your pack and got to work on you. We used it all ... sorry about that." It sure tasted like it.

If Craghead could have held his booze we'd still be there ... never known the truth again. I went to the window, I still wasn't right, it took most of what was left of the night to really come down out of it. I took great gulps of air and worked on it.

The countryside echoed and squeaked and splashed with those irrigation wheels. The people that worked on them were singing in the dark ... maybe they just worked until they fell off and died. More phosphates in the water. A final contribution. Still, they were happy.

There were a couple of hoverers moving about over the fields. They seemed to be running south towards the glowing Crystal Mountains, but I couldn't make any-thing of that. Those trees ... blossoming in the gardens ... I looked real hard, blinked a couple of times and they were the same stuff as the thicket. There were a couple of magnolias, but they were pretty tatty ... there were a lot more of the Alien plants.

I looked further and the whole scene shifted and be-came different. The things they were growing ... they weren't like anything that started on earth ... they didn't rattle or rustle in the night breeze the way canes should. They *sounded* rather ... like muted gongs ... it was part of the music the place had.

You could see the odd clump of a pink stuff standing down there amongst it all ... spread about the light-reflecting grid that was the canals. I wondered why someone didn't grease those water wheels – then it struck

me that labour didn't matter there ... there was a con-
tempt for effort and work that was total. It couldn't
matter less what people did.

There was one of those canals near the house. I went
down the creaking stairs, out in the open and bathed in
it. At first I thought it was ordinary water, but it wasn't.
Thicker somehow – almost jelly in places ... it was
sticky too. It cleaned me up all the same.

As I washed my hair I found that flower that Cristan
had put there. I pulled it out and it hurt. I yelped and
had a look at the thing.

About a quarter inch of scalp had come with it. The
damn thing had been taking root. It was a good thing it
hadn't reached the bone.

It wasn't a flower either, of course. It was made of
that thicket stuff again, some of that pink stuff about it
too ... almost white ... like a bud. I cut it open with
my knife and it had a half-formed eye and communicator unit in it. I threw it in the canal.

I crossed back across the dead grey dust that had
been dewy lawn the night before and went in through
the house. I opened a couple of doors there and the
people inside looked well enough, smiling asleep with
their arms round each other. I looked at the control
units and the carapaces and wondered why I hadn't
noticed them before. I wondered if it mattered anyway.
I mean – if you're happy what does it matter? How the
hell do you know you're happy anyway?

We found the Riders and got them awake too. Craghead made them bring it all up by stamping on their
bellies. He had a short way with problems like that. One
came out OK but the other was too far gone. We should
have thought of them sooner. We saw him a bit later,
happy as a little boy, working on a water wheel. As far
as I know he never made it out.

When the sun was up and we felt a bit better we ate
some beans out of my pack. I didn't have a lot left, we
sure weren't going to eat any of the stuff they fed you
there.

By that time there were people shifting about down-stairs so we went on down. I was worried about what they might do if they found out tney'd failed, but we smiled and they smiled and no one seemed to notice. I don't think they even knew they were doped themselves let alone what they'd tried to do to us.

Cristan offered me one of his cigarettes. I refused and rolled up one of my own. His hair was a light carapace and the flower was one of those eyes that Wardens have sometimes. Not that that was a surprise.

"You liked them yesterday," he said. He was almost accusing me, I think I hurt his feelings.

"Happy days," said the girl and it was OK again.

They offered us food too. We didn't take any of course, although I did taste some on the end of my finger. It was just that same pap they put out in the north – it only seemed better last night. It seemed they put those drugs out in combinations ... like one masked and backed the other – so it worked out the further south you came the more you got – which figured. Now, when we went out, those perfumes gave me a head-ache.

It was Cristan that took us out. He said we were to meet the Fathers and the girl said yes before I could stop her. I mean, it was obvious the Fathers were prob-ably the Aliens. Aliens pretending to be good guys – benefactors who cared for their people – they'd sure hate anyone who could really see them ... and they wouldn't be like Cristan! They'd know ... they'd *know!*

But the girl had said yes and we were on the way. Well ... I suppose I was curious too ... anyway, now I was back in reality, I was hating again. I might get a chance to kill a couple. Pay them back for some of that ice, make up a little for the Defeat.

We drove down the serried clumps of the cane stuff. It was ugly really – nothing lush about it. In spite of all the water it looked like dry, sparse hair, slightly curled. I guess it must have come from a really wet planet.

Kind of blue-grey it was ... with occasional marker

109

columns of that pink stuff standing up in it. The people there were pretty ragged and not very clean after all ... they all looked healthy though, which was a change from the north. I guess the ill ones didn't survive too long. The terrible thing was they were so happy ... working themselves dead for something they only thought they were getting.

It got lighter as we got near the Mountains. Even in that bright morning it got lighter. We weren't going straight there – it was like going through a maze of canes ... but all the time – each time we looked – we were getting nearer those shining heights. I doubt we could have turned away if we wanted to . and I did ... I *did*. Part of my mind was screaming with terror.

Then we were past the final cane bed and the Mountains started almost at once. It was crystals. Small ones at first ... some of them loose ... maybe a foot or two across ... there were even smaller ones, they crunched on each other under our feet as we walked on in

Six-sided. The tops like six-sided pyramids. They were transparent ... light echoed and reflected in them ... there were flashing rainbows and pure colours ... it was wonderland

"Aching beauty," said Cristan. "Who would live but under the light of this place? The words of God carved in the pure crystal of reality ... our Fathers gathered order there. The ordering and alteration of crass nature ... the ordering of made things ... the making of man to conform to happiness ..."

There was a path up there, a stairway rather, the steps formed by horizontal crystals

Soon the crystals were getting really big – nine maybe ten feet around ... the whole Mountains were made of them ... piled and grown on top of each other. The light got to be almost unbearable. We screwed our eyes and made it as well as we could ... tears streamed down ... you could hardly see. The whole thing was incandescent with sun. There was a sort of grain running in the way the crystals lay – like in wood sometimes – it seemed to direct what happened to the light ... controlled it.

110

Reflected and refracted the right wavelengths down into Happy Land – that's what the girl said.

Altogether it took most of the day to get anywhere near the crest. There was only the one way to go, there were no alternatives ... just the one stairway hemmed in by big crystals. We staggered on, half blinded, sweating ... confined in those glassy thirty-foot walls.

CHAPTER TWELVE

It was so *hot*. Hot and somehow constricted ... even under that great sky it felt constricted. It was neverland. Rainbows and all illusions. Glimpses of landscape ... mirages and visions ... angular lights and splitting shadows. There was nothing alive up there ... no birds ... no animals. Sometimes we tried to talk – to make it more bearable ... it was the empty chatter of monkeys so mostly we said nothing. I suppose in the end there's never much to say.

Sunset was beautiful. Even I saw that. All those fragmented reds and oranges slowly giving way to the last mauves and violets ... all uncertain and changing and lightful.

When we got more onto the crest we couldn't see anything of the surrounding countryside. On either side there was purple night. The Mountains themselves were light. You couldn't see anything else for the glare ... except maybe the odd light from houses or perhaps a reflected glint from the canals. It was strange to walk on a light source ... it made everything look crazy. The girl with her four breasts lit up from underneath for example ... her face too.

After a while I realized the canyon we were walking into had got roofed over and what we were in was a cave now ... a sort of slot in the Mountain.

It wasn't dark in there of course – the place was all flooded with the Mountain's light. Cristan was impatient too – you still couldn't help liking the poor guy – so we went on.

There was music there too. A humming ... like of pipes ... a soft and pleasant sound. Eerie it was ... eerie.

"It's the crystals," said the girl when she saw me puzzled. "Now the sun's gone the air in here has begun to contract ... air from outside's come in to fill the volume ... the breeze is sounding round the crystals. In the morning – when the sun is warm again – it'll happen the other way."

The music got louder as we went further. You could feel the breeze behind us so I guess the girl was right. It was like the crystal place was sucking us in – it made you uneasy.

Then the crystals got bigger, reaching from floor to ceiling, the cave opened up too and the music stopped. Mind – you couldn't really tell anything much in that confusing haze of light. There were smaller crystals too, only inches or only feet long, reaching from the ceiling like daggers, or sprouting from the floor or the walls.

The light was funny, I couldn't tell if it was getting darker or brighter. It was like it was and it wasn't. When the sun had gone and we got deeper the reds and yellows disappeared and all the light was in blues and whites and greys ... violets and indigos. It was dimmer too ... then again you knew it was hurting your eyes the way light did when it was too bright.

"Actinic," said the girl. "A special environment." She was whispering but her voice echoed and rustled all around that great space.

When you looked you could see other things in there besides crystals. One time or another we all thought we saw figures or something move. Then we thought they were our reflections and I guess maybe some of them were – we sometimes saw ourselves repeated and imaged in blueness, shadowed and moving into distance. Others weren't us though – there were mysterious figures, some of them in those blank blue helmets I knew so well. They just stood there, deep in the crystals ... Maybe they were looking at us, but you couldn't tell ... maybe they were miles away, or not there at all ... just images and possibilities in the Mountain. None of them moved, after a little we began to ignore them. It was that sort of place.

Suddenly there was an end in front of us. There were holes in it though ... angular crannies leading away to remoteness. At first we thought it was some sort of turning, but there was no way out of it, it was a dead end. I looked at the girl.

"We go on," she said. "We can't stop now." I didn't fancy it myself, crawling down those challenging crannies with no way to turn.

We stood there trying to will each other down in that shifting light. I don't know what would have happened if the wall hadn't gurgled.

Down in those crooked spaces something moved. A greyed pinkness glowed down there in the blue. Then it moved and was coming forward. It pulsed – it filled the whole of the space there. The glugging sound came nearer – louder. We stood petrified. It was the most horrible thing I ever saw. You'd have been scared too. All I could think about was flies. Craghead started to run, he got two paces then found he had to halt and watch. He stared, eyes wide, mouth open to snarl, his teeth parted. Hell – we all felt like that.

That pinkness filled the crannies – it filled the world – all my awareness. I wanted to be sick again . . . it was like being hypnotized. The place was filled with perfume . . . it was that same stuff as in the Happy Land . . . it sure wasn't flowers.

Then the pink went white. Flickered, went white and bubbled a little. Quite suddenly I couldn't take it any more. I reached for my gun. Cristan hit me like a battering ram.

"No!" he screamed. "You shall not hurt our Fathers!"

I rolled on the floor. Cristan's hands were on my throat, crystals dug in my back.

I clubbed him on the side of the head. If it hadn't been for the carapace I'd have killed him. As it was it just loosened his hands for a second.

I managed to get up. He came at me again. I kneed him in the groin. I kept doing that . . . his face writhed with agony. He kept coming and had my throat again.

I dug in my chin and kept kneeing him in the crotch. I tried for his eyes with my thumbs. It didn't make a bit

114

of difference, he still half choked me. My head started to pound – my vision dimmed. I was going.

Craghead saved me. He grabbed the Rider's rifle and swung it like an axe at Cristan's head.

Cristan went down. His head was all bloody ... that thin carapace was knocked all one-sided. There was blood oozing all underneath it ... one eye was all swollen and there was blood beneath the lid.

He spat out some teeth, tried to get up, collapsed onto his face and lay still. His legs kicked once.

I fought for breath. That extra eye that I thought was a flower rolled and popped ... then turned the colour of milk. I was still fighting for breath. It was horrible.

"What?" said Cristan. "Mother ... where am I? Where have the Fathers gone?" he paused. "It hurts. It hurts!"

"You have separated our man," said the Pink Wall.

We whirled on it. Forgot the moaning Cristan and stared at the Wall.

There were holes there ... they blurred and became mouths. Those bubbles were mouths now! Many of them ... shifting and wet mouths. Sure – you expect odd things from Aliens – but these mouths, they were so ... so *human.* That thick scent redoubled ... it was horrible. All those horrible wet mouths.

It went on talking to us ... saying something ... I don't know. After a moment you couldn't tell which of those bubbled wet mouths was speaking. Not one of them ever finished a whole sentence – it would shift and the Wall would be talking about the same thing somewhere else. Sometimes they moved on the surface too ... maybe merged or divided ... they existed in depth. One behind the other – and there were images and reflections too.

Cristan was trying to get up again. We stood there and he moaned at our feet.... Craghead was sobbing with fear ... he was a frightened man – so he should have been.

"Mother," said Cristan, "please tell me where I am ... I can't think ... *help me* ...! It's dark ..."

"Quietly, rest now," said the girl. "Don't struggle ... don't move." She had her hands on his shoulders, holding him, but she was looking at the Wall.

"*Ah,*" said part of the Wall. "*My/their man. A family man. Who/what has dared separate our/their communication?*"

"*CRISTAN!*" shouted all the mouths together. "*Why have you separated? Why are you no longer part?*"

"Alien!" screamed Cristan. He struggled to get up. "Alien will kill my Fathers! The women and children!" Young Craghead grunted and moved to hold him down.

"*Why are we/they bothered to be physical? Why has true communication ceased?*"

"*That ... one ... that ICE LOVER ... that one the YOUNG CRAGHEAD ... they/he have ceased the contact ... that one part of my/their thing Cristan ...!*"

"*Wicked, unbeautiful, unhappy – so we/they make these mouths.*" The Wall was talking amongst its mouths, it was very confusing. Cristan was struggling all the time.

"*CRISTAN!*" said all the Wall again. Pretty soon it took everyone except me to hold him down. He fought like wild. I kept out of it, carefully moved back and kept my gun on the Wall.

"Alien!" Cristan threw the girl off. Craghead rolled away. "*Kill the ingrate monsters! Protect our/my entirety!*" He didn't have a chance.

Craghead dragged two of his arms up behind him. I heard the bones creak. The Rider was in there somewhere too. Cristan was a horrible sight ... that splintered loose carapace with the blood oozing under it ... there was blood everywhere, but he was still fighting.

"*It is too much to lose,*" said part of the Wall. "*Fight! Lay down your small all for us/them!*"

"*An effort! A final effort for final triumph!*"

"*For our/their entirety! Kill the beastly Aliens!*"

Cristan redoubled his effort. Those delicate secondary hands clawed at the girl's eyes. When she pulled her head back they raced to her belt and snatched the pistol there.

116

Craghead swore and lunged forward grabbing at the weapon. He yelped as Cristan bit him. Later Craghead found teeth marks all up his thigh – but he got the wrist with the pistol.

Cristan twisted his hand so he could shoot at me. He wasn't trying for the people that held him – he was after me. I was the one with the gun on the Wall.

I moved out of the arc of the pistol. Cristan started shooting anyway.

The shots were enormous in that cave. They drowned even what the Wall was saying ... white bullet holes splashed into the hard clear walls. Then about a yard deep they exploded into white crazed spheres blank in the clearness. Hard white dust filled the air ... chips and splinters rattled on the floor.

I got further left and dodged the shots. Altogether he fired maybe six times before Craghead crushed his wrist and he dropped the pistol. Even then he fought on. Screaming agony he wormed across the floor to try again for the pistol.

I moved and kicked it away. Craghead kept hitting and hitting him. The girl held his legs as hard as she could. Then, suddenly Cristan was dead.

"Mother ... entirety ..." he said. Then he screamed "ALIEN!" and died

His back was arched like a bow – his good arms stretched rigid, his eyes started out ... his mouth dragged open. There was more blood from his tongue, he'd practically bitten it through. Young Craghead sat back on the floor, the girl got slowly up. When you looked at Cristan ... he was so puny and gentle-looking ... but he sure took a lot of killing.

"*Ah,*" said the Wall. "*It is ceased.*"

We stood in the perfume and powder smoke and looked at the blood seeping through Cristan's fists. Someone's breath sobbed in the silence.

"*Now,*" said the Wall. "*Why are you not of the entity?*"

"*Why have you come here with weapons when all we/they desire is peace?*"

117

"How can you exist without the entirety? How is it you are not part of the conformity? How can this be?"

"We are here to see you," said the girl. "We have avoided your traps and delusions."

"Individuality is not natural. You cannot be. All should be part of the entirety – live in the exchange of ideas."

"All is part of whole. You are Alien and should not be."

"Alien?" snarled Craghead. "You're Alien – we're Human!" So it was – but that was a laugh coming from him!

"Alien ... Alien," said the Wall. *"This is our/their world. As it has always – or almost always – been ... as nearly all are. Perhaps it was even our/their original world ... It is so covered in time we/they cannot remember or be sure. Either or neither ... perhaps or perhaps not ... how can there be any certainty in such matters. Hypothetical ... so how can it matter. We/they have entirety in many worlds and many consciousnesses ... they/it are all ours/theirs."*

"It's *our* world." Craghead sounded sullen.

"Not significant," said the Wall. *"Home is where you fill."*

"We/they would only live in peace. Leave us/them be ..."

The Wall surface was suddenly more agitated. The changes and shifts became quicker. It bulged and swayed ... mouths disappeared and bubbled back ... forms twisted and re-formed.

"You got to go," said young Craghead. No one paid any notice. That boy was a *fool* – what did he think it'd do – disappear in a flash of maroon light?

"Why?" said the girl. "Why did you subjugate those people? Do what you did to them?"

"Necessary," said the Wall. *"We/they needed them ... needed them to be head of. It was natural they should be part of our/their entity and our/their minions ... the entirety."*

"We/they knew we/they could do better. There was so much . . . death." The Wall said "death" like it didn't like the taste of the word. Still . . . who does?

"What will you/it do to us? Peace . . . make peace . . . ? Help us/them to survive?"

"If you're so keen on peace why did Cristan try to kill us?"

"We/they will give you immortality in our collective conscious . . . ?"

"Individuality frightens us/them . . . we/they were frightened."

"I/we/they have illness . . . there is pain . . . ache . . ."

I started to wonder why the Aliens weren't trying to get us right then. I looked around and poked about with my gun. You never know what might be creeping up on you. There was nothing though.

"We/they want . . . mercy . . . help . . . that we/they may survive."

"I/we/they are sentient . . . great intelligence . . . help us/them survive . . . ?"

"No power . . ." said another mouth there. I may be wrong – but I thought I saw small sharp teeth in it. *"Hate men . . . hate individuals . . . cannot use our/my/their weapons here . . ."*

I could though. I wondered what I'd kill if I started shooting right into that pink Wall. Small crystals began to grow on the Wall.

"No – crystals cannot protect us/them against Ice Lover's weapon. Tell them . . . show all . . . we/they are worthy to survive . . . show that for the man things' mercy."

I saw a vision then. Faintly first . . . I always knew it was a dream . . . they couldn't hold me like they could Cristan . . . I was never fooled like he was.

It was an ocean. Enormous . . . thicker than water . . . rocks on broad beaches. There were shellfish . . . like mussels . . . pink – in my vision they kept changing into great clumps of mussels like I'd seen once in the north. They weren't really though . . . small red things that lived in white shells . . . feeding on the thick things that lived in that ocean. Animals . . . they breathed with wiry gills when the tide came there.

Then I guess they skipped a few thousand million years of evolution and the ocean was gone . . . maybe it wasn't even the same place. The shellfish were still there – but like all one . . . they were a brain now. Each little creature had maybe a few hundred or thousand nerve fibres . . . individually they were nothing, but they weren't individual – they had communication . . . *connections*.

The whole colony . . . million upon teeming million . . . it was one entity. They'd made their own rocks . . . grown those crystals . . . lived within them . . . they had animals who worked for them, each with a small insert of the brain stuff. They controlled them . . . radio or something that wasn't quite that . . . a product of the crystals. They had canals . . feeding those reed lungs of theirs . . they stretched over across and across and around their planet. They had all the world, they had vast intelligence.

Then more aeons had passed. I saw the Aliens spread all across the galaxy. Those great intelligences could do anything . . . they had infinite time – as a cell died, so another grew to its place – they were immortal. They were everywhere . . . they bent worlds to their image and their will . . . it was wonderful. They were wonderful.

Then it released me . . . there was a *feeling* . . . an infinite languor, a nostalgia for that Alien past. I was back in the cave. Maybe a second had passed.

The Wall was really boiling now. Seething and maybe fighting itself. Mouths came and went. It was chaos.

"But use men for what they do best. It is their natural purpose in the entirety. To serve we/us. Men kill well. they work well, use them in our/their plan."

"Serve me/us! Ask them mercy! This is our/their world . . . the glory of galactic movement! All worlds are the great entirety!"

"But the thing men do best! BEWARE! We/they should make peace . . ."

"Better cease than ask mercy!"

"Men! How dare you stand! Individual ... indecent! Our/their power encompasses you!"

"Please ... request ... do not harm us/them ... we/they are frightened ... alone amongst intelligence so individual ... so lonely ..."

The Pink had gone. It came back ... the mouths were smaller – less distinct. Some hung slack. There weren't only mouths now ... random forms came and went ... circles and not circles ... waving things ... smoothness and roughness ... misformed things ... and crude colours waving ... images and indistinct distinctions that were somehow sick ... dotty patterns.

"Great truth," murmured the Wall with all its parts. *"Ultimate truth from our/their ages ... and brilliance. LISTEN!"*

"There's black and white ... a particular red for given green, there's rough and smooth and nothing in between! Moving and standing still in all the wondering thoughts and musics of imperfect spheres ... right and we/they are never wrong."

"Fear and hate ... we/they fear everything ..."

"It's mad! said young Craghead. "Like my father ... gaga!"

"Don't give it human values," said the girl. "But you could be right. Sick with years and power ... it's been too long. Once it'd have been an entity ... a coherent intelligence ... a common nervous system. Now it's diseased ... breaking down."

Something was happening to the Wall.

"Kill me/us!" it said. *"Too late ... show mercy ..."*

A tendril of Pink sneaked out. It curled round the pistol Cristan had left on the floor. Just like an Alien – say one thing and mean another! They were almost human.

"We/they kill! Be master! We/they are your God!"

I pulled myself together. Part of the Wall had given up – the rest wanted to fight.

I started shooting. I blew a great hole where the pistol was and followed that with four more.

The mouths seemed to be screaming.

"You won't kill it like that," said the girl. I wondered calmly how she knew a thing like that. I grabbed the radiation grenades out of my pack.

Those first four bullet craters had almost closed. Mouths spat the bullets onto the floor. Contemptuous it was . . . contemptuous.

I shot another hole into the wall, pulled the cap off the grenade and hurled it in as far as I could. I did it again and again. I sowed grenades all over and into that writhing surface. I used almost all I had . . . then I began to run. The Wall was screaming . . . the cave echoed . . . I knew I'd hurt it anyway.

I turned and saw the Pink contract back down the crannies. The grenades went with it . . . imbedded and carried back.

I had the last cap in my hand. I held it towards where the radiation burst would be. If I was going to get maybe a lethal dose then I wanted to know.

The cave walls pulsed maroon light. Deep down there. Again and again and again.

The indicator in my hand didn't move. The Alien had stopped the lot . . . except the light not a scrap of radiation had reached us.

There was some moaning and then silence. It was uncanny after all the noise and shouting.

CHAPTER THIRTEEN

SOMEWHERE something was dripping. We were looking into each other's eyes. We were poised to run for it if we had to.

"I believe," said the girl slowly. "I believe you really hurt it. I do believe it's dead . . . or dying . . ."

We started moving again, breathing and looking about us. There wasn't anything else, no sound, no nothing. Craghead braced himself, he walked across and peered into where the Wall was.

"It's clear," he said. I went up more slowly, gathering the indicator caps off the grenades as I went. They all said "zero" so I went and looked with him.

There were some shreds of Pink down there. Like meat. Like a burst balloon. Water – maybe – dripped from them . . . almost as we watched what was left dissolved and ran away down between the crystals. There were bits of grenade casing down there and hundreds of small white things that looked like big cartridge cases. It was all wet and it smelled. A long time seemed to pass.

"I really do," said the girl at my elbow. "I believe you've killed them." I hadn't seen her come, I seemed to remember her saying something like that before. It was so *quiet* there. I kept shivering and having to turn round, but there was never anything. More time passed.

"Maybe they're *all* dead," said the girl. "It'd explain things if they were. Think of it – those we talked to – the last remnants of millions upon piled millions. The first galactic race . . . perhaps it was a galactic intelligence – think of *that!*"

"I bet they filled all this." Young Craghead was looking reflective, leaning on the crystals there, frowning a little as he thought.

"The whole damn Mountain," said the girl. "A

palace. I believe you're right. Millions upon millions . . . a girdle of Aliens all round the world . . . and all dead now. Remarkable they had such power still . . . it was breaking though. Those brambles and stuff . . . the earth plants . . . they'd never have allowed that if they could have stopped it. There'd be a minimum – the thinking would function quite well right up until there were just too few creatures . . . then it'd break down – like we saw. Senescence!" I guess they all had that vision the Aliens gave me.

About that time the sun must have come up because the light brightened and got more natural. The air began to move the way the girl said it would. As the breeze built up it moaned around the crystals like reed pipes. It was like a dirge or flies buzzing. Another of my damn symbols . . . sad in memory of the Aliens. I started wondering if they'd died one death or a million separate ones in all that dissolving consciousness.

The girl said we should check that place. Look deeper and make sure they were all dead and the world was free again. She was right but I didn't want to go down there. It was still only just dawning on me that we'd won.

We followed the canting, sloping crazy crannies into the deeps. We didn't find a thing. Nothing alive I mean. There were hundreds and millions of those little bone cartridge cases – they crunched under our feet, in places they were yards deep . . . the corners between the crystals were packed thick with them. They were what was left of one hell of a lot of Aliens . . . the last vestiges of their shellfish origins . . . and now, at their end, all that was left. That actinic light of theirs ended too, gave way to ordinary daylight reflected and incandescent all through the Mountains. I guess that without their control even the crystals didn't work properly.

In the end we were on a ledge overlooking a vast cavern place half filled with slushy water stuff. It sure stank, a sort of mixture between the Aliens' perfume and the stink of their corruption. We stood on a thick carpet of shells and looked down on the stuff. It was all

124

that was left of them ... they'd died, rotted and run down there ... it was all that was left.

We none of us felt very clever right then. I mean, death ... the end of all that, killing the last sick fragments of a once great thing. I felt like a jackal ... a sort of dog come down from the hills to rip the last life from some sick and weakened lion. I wasn't proud of it.

"I think we could almost call it mercy," said the girl. "It ... it was dying anyway ... they couldn't have survived long ... it's not their world. We saved them a lingering death ..."

I guess she was trying to make me feel good. I mean, I'd really had it – had enough of killing. I'd just killed millions ... it ought to have been enough for anyone. It was my old downswing again.

Anyway, everything that was owing had been paid. A shadow was gone from the land. Maybe they deserved to die. How would I know? I'm no judge. I made myself think of the modifications, the girl's four breasts, Craghead's piebald skin and God knows what else besides. Now they were dead ... those creatures that perverted humanity for their own purpose ... that sort deserve about all they get. I guess I felt better then. In the end I just felt sad.

There was another thing too. It was uneasy ... somehow wrong. An anticlimax ... too easy. Even then I thought it was too easy. A premonition, maybe.

Then we left that sad lake and turned back for the surface. There wasn't much to say.

When we came to where Cristan was we found a shallow cranny and shoved him in. Then we blocked it with bits of broken crystal and Alien shells. It was as good a place as any to be dead in.

We must have been deeper than I thought because it was dark again by the time we got out onto the crest. We were all pretty quiet and the girl was still trying to cheer us up.

125

"It's sad," she said. "We've won but it's sad. All that superior intelligence ruined and dying mad. We just did what we're supposed to do. It is *our* world, remember. No regrets..." I won't say she completely cleared our minds, it still didn't feel the release and victory it really was. Maybe it was that vision of their history they'd given me ... that working on my mind.

We didn't go right down onto the plain. No one fancied that now it was night and the Mountains had died and stopped giving light. The girl found a ledge and she spent the night there looking out over the darkness all around. She was singing something sad to herself. I wished I had a drink. I wanted to cry.

It was odd ... those Mods, Craghead and the girl ... they were the ones who the Aliens had really worked on. They at least should have been happy ... they were the ones who should have hated ... but they were just as sad as I was. They're a sentimental lot Mods, weak-minded. Then it struck me they'd never known what it was like to be a Free Man, so why should I break my heart. I went to sleep.

It was snowing in the morning. After a few minutes it was a real blizzard and the wind was really *hitting*. Howling and thundering all round the crystal peaks. Then it changed to rain and half an hour after that the sun was shining.

We began to move along the crest to where those steps were and we could get down again. The girl said now the Aliens weren't controlling the weather any more it'd go mad for a while until it settled to a natural balance. She reckoned the ice caps would move back to where they were supposed to be, but that'd take a few years to happen. It sure hasn't happened yet!

You could see right out across the Happy Land. There were maybe a dozen separate storms going on down there, they stretched away as far as you could see east and west. The ridge was mostly above all that and we watched the sunlit great boiling cloud masses moving in the coppery air. Sometimes they merged, sometimes they pulled apart in vast churning cliffs and indigo shadows beneath ... splitting cracks of lightning there. It was real power ... the atmosphere raged with energy. Far west a couple of whirlwinds spiralled and cut through the cane beds

For one moment I saw the Thicket white in sunlight against the black-shadowed Border. It was a mirage of some sort – something in the wild variations of the tortured air – but the whole thing was brought close. I saw the metal plain brought up and held there too. Oval it was ... long and slender-seeming, very gently curving up in the middle part – then it waved ... wavered ... and was gone. The girl smiled when I told her – she explained all about how mirages worked to me – how you couldn't trust them and it was probably the sky bent into the landscape. The weather had closed in so she didn't see it for herself. I didn't know what to think.

We went on down. Sometimes we froze and sometimes we baked ... soaked with rain and stung with hail. When it was raining you could see the crystals broken and breaking down. They seemed soluble now, the rain worked on them like acid, as they decomposed they became soft and slippery. I guess that was why the Aliens controlled the climate so rigidly – why they had such control of their fluids. A lot of things would change now the Aliens were gone.

Rain beat on Cristan's truck when we found it. It was a downpour like you couldn't breathe – the truck had a halo of rain spray a yard all around it. When we got in the drumming on the roof was fantastic.

We dried off as best we could and the girl drove off north as fast as she dared through the grey rain curtains. We went north bursting through the canes until we hit a canal then followed that until we struck the north road. The canes were decaying too ... softening to pulp in the rain.

There were people there still working as if nothing had happened, there were others just running and falling about – to or from what I couldn't guess and I don't suppose they could either. Men were cutting canes in one

127

place. Loading sodden bales of the stuff onto their trucks. I got out my gun and wiped it dry.

There was rain and water everywhere – nature making up for lost time I suppose. It was sure wet though.

There were some guys tried to kill us. Wardens of course ... the girl said the Alien grafts in their heads would live as long as they did, but that two or three ounces of Alien weren't enough to be dangerous. It was nothing to worry about and there wasn't anything we could do about it either. We shot them down all the same.

There were a lot of people who'd made it to Cristan's town, to get out of the rain, maybe. They sat slumped and soaking and looked at us with great dark eyes, they didn't move. Craghead wanted to lob in radiation grenades but the girl said there'd been enough killing. We went north faster than ever on the half-flooded road.

At the Thicket the storms had quietened so you could see pretty well. The earth plants had suddenly got going there, the brambles showed green leaves and the grass was sprouting like it was spring. There were birds all over the Thicket, all feeding on whatever it was made of. Our engine scared them off so you could see their feet and beak marks all over it ... millions of them. Some of the birds had eaten too much and there were foxes after them.

"A corpse," said Craghead. You could see how the thing had collapsed and the skin had wrinkled where it couldn't get tight enough. It hadn't even had a skin before.

"It would have been like a hide," said the girl. "Think of the canals like blood and veins ... stomach juices ... those canes like lungs somehow. And the thinking parts the Aliens themselves ... using the Mountains like a skeleton. They needed men – or something – to clear the cane beds ... and for Wardens – for protection. It could have spread all over the world if it'd gone right for them. Think of what that would have looked like from space! Don't worry about killing them – it – Ice Lover ... you did right."

128

On the other side we found the girl's truck and changed to that. Don't ask me why ... but it was sure good to hear that offbeat fan again. Plants were in blossom on the way ... and they were real ones this time.

The Borderland wasn't a lot different from last time. It was mud now – all that black dust soil had just turned to sticky mud. There were some people wandering about, walking in circles it seemed like. They weren't going anywhere, like they'd lost their purpose in life.

On the metal part, in a dry period, we saw a dust devil come screwing and sucking from the mud onto the metal. It was black while it was on the mud, then it turned red from the new rust when it reached the iron. A hoverer went over about then, I wondered where *he* was going.

When we got out of the mud and into the first beech trees there were some Wardens sitting there. Not doing anything – just sitting staring at each other. They hardly saw us as we passed, sitting there, the light amber in their carapaces. I guess they probably sat there forever waiting for someone to tell them something. There were damaged places in the trees, some had been torn down ... there were leaves on the ground where they'd been torn off by the hail. There were people hiding in the woods, the ones that were thinking ran when they saw us coming. No one shot at us, which was a change.

Things had sure taken a beating ... nothing was going to be the same again ... you couldn't even start thinking about what the effects might be.

Craghead's place, the gate of the Enclosure, looked pretty good to me. Maybe the walls were cleaner from all the rain – one high place looked like it had been struck by lightning. Everybody seemed scared by what had happened, jumpy, but they let us through when they saw the girl. We hadn't met any scouting Riders like I had when I got there first. All the Enclosure was filled with sheltering Mods.

The girl drove quickly through the crowd and right up to the shaft with the man-elevator. We heard people discussing what they'd do to the people who stirred up all the trouble with the Aliens. They seemed frightened, in a nasty mood, so we went down the shaft as quickly as we could.

Far below, beyond the treadmill and in the sound of dripping water there were lights. I remembered the engines Rutherford had been building there ... but then I saw the lights were beyond even that. They'd built another treadmill alongside the first to reach the new engines and below.

There was a lot of activity in the shaft. Shadows moved and bounced on the walls, there was shouting and movement, wreaths and banks of hot steam all the way down.

When I hit the first level the girl was talking to some of the Mods there. It was sure good to be back amongst even those guys ... at least they possessed themselves. They were the way Mods should be, dangerous and well-armed. It was good to see everybody with a gun again.

"Down," the girl told me. "We've got to go on down. The pumpman emptied the lower level and Craghead's down there. We have to go down."

We went to where they'd cut a hole in the grid and walked down the wooden steps to where the treadmills were. We stepped onto the lower man-elevator and it carried us down through steam and heat, past Rutherford's new engine towards the furthest lights. As we went a wooden box full of filthy mud swayed past us into the blaze of lit steam above.

You could see what they meant, the walls had sure been shot up. There were scars and scorch marks torn in it just about all the way down. There was one place where there'd been some sort of rail things set once, but there wasn't much of them left, only a few twisted rods and holes where things had been fastened.

At the bottom we stepped onto a wooden grid all lashed and pegged along one of the walls. Below again there were some Mods working in mud and slime shovelling the stuff through big sieves and then sending it up in the wooden boxes. There was another box where they put the things they found in the mud. There were skulls there – with and without carapaces – old helmets ... bright red with deep-water rust or blackened with the slime, there were shell cases too, scores of spent bullets ... great chunks of broken concrete. There were weapons too, but they were too far gone to learn much from. A guard there directed us along a tunnel to where we'd find Craghead.

It was pretty clammy down there, a lot of it had been cleaned up – they must have shifted a load of mud ... you could see the stain where it had been six or seven feet up the walls. Some of the side tunnels were still silted almost to the roof, thick water was still draining from there. The whole place stank. Great drooping festooned shrouds of slime hung from the ceiling where it was too high to reach easily.

As far as I could see the layout was much the same as the level above except there was less subdivision and it somehow seemed bigger. There were some circular holes drilled in the floor and roof, the ones in the floor were filled with mud and you couldn't see what the roof ones were.

Pretty soon we came to a big chamber with a lot of guys working in it, shovelling and sieving. There'd been fighting there too. The walls were scarred and there were bones about. One of the Mods said how Rutherford had told them to leave everything exactly as they found it. It was curious how the bones were in line, in groups of maybe six or a dozen, almost as if they'd been laid out in some meaningful pattern. A sacrifice perhaps, or a code. They'd been pretty well-armed – not a sword amongst them – they all had guns.

The head shoveller said that Rutherford reckoned that's just what it was – a code – that he might be able to figure out what happened from how the bones lay. Like an augury the shoveller thought ... but I didn't think Rutherford would have meant that.

Under where Craghead's place would have been there was an even bigger hall. I guess that was why he'd

131

moved down. He already had his dais and his throne there. They'd kindled a fire for him and were working on heating the place up. I guess it was the same chimney as above, they seemed to be having trouble getting the fire to burn right. There were braziers everywhere but it was still cold and damp and Craghead was coughing plenty. I thought of suggesting he move back up where it was warmer and the air was better, but then I thought how miserable he looked so I kept my mouth shut.

The girl went up and reported to Craghead. You could see he wasn't really interested though, he wasn't understanding even. When she told him the Aliens were dead he brightened up, but when she explained there was no plunder and it had all washed away he lost interest again. He hadn't understood yet, he hadn't seen the possibilities, it was too big for him. I went to find Old Rutherford.

He was busy with some shovellers when I found him. They had water trays fixed up in a smaller room off the big one and they were washing and laying out things that they'd found. He left it when I showed up and listened while I told him what had happened and how we'd finished the Aliens.

"Aye ... that's about what it must have been," he said when I'd finished. "Best thought of as a single body. It's a sad thing ... strange that something like that would ever get old ... all those little animals should have kept on replacing themselves ... it should never get senile. What a mind it must have been ... what a mind!"

"It could be pretty nasty if Craghead turns out boss," I ventured after a while – I'd had enough of how sad it was the Aliens were dead. "If he's ruler and there's no brake on his power, I mean."

"Aye," Rutherford frowned. "I wonder what he'll do. All that tied his kingdom together was fear of the Aliens. He'll have to find something else to be frightened of ... to persecute. Probably Free Men ... he's always hated us. And if Craghead ends up ruling the world – it might come off – just think what that'd be like ... just exactly the same ... he's as senile as the Aliens were." Old

132

Rutherford could be pretty bitter when there was no one about.

He got excited when I told him about the metal plain. I asked him why – it seemed important to me as well, but I couldn't quite figure out why. Anyway, to me the big thing was that we'd killed the Aliens.

"Don't you see? It's obvious what it is – it's got to be the Aliens' spaceship! Only a starship could be that big. More than half buried – it would have to be that big. Do you see now? We'll just have to go to it!" He thought for a second. "Don't talk about it any more – we'll try and keep it to ourselves ... among Free Men." It was obvious when you thought about it. Of course the Aliens had to have a ship someplace – and we'd have to have a look at it. Even I could see we stood to learn a lot.

"How is it here?" I asked. He had to finish this job first, I knew. "Plenty of toys for Craghead?" I never saw a guy like Craghead for collecting ancient junk he didn't know how to use. If we had to we could sell him the idea of opening and exploring the ship for what we might find in it.

"Well, we've sieved a lot of mud," said Rutherford. "There are a lot of dead men. Come and look at this." He led me to a pile of skulls they had there. "Notice anything?"

"There sure are enough," I said.

"There's not a carapace!" said Rutherford triumphantly. "Not one! All Free Men. The fight here must have been long before the Defeat. This place must have been a base ... a bunker ... we can learn a lot about how things were then."

"Those patterns the bones are laid in back there," I said. "Those rows. It's like they were in those caves we found in the Crystal Mountains. They went pretty deep too ..."

Rutherford stood up very straight and reached in his pocket to show me something.

"What do you make of these? Have you seen anything like this?" He held out his hand full of the shell

133

tubes we found when the Alien died. The cylinders that held the pinkness. They were very stained from the mud but you could see what they were. "There are tons," he said. "Tons!"

I told him what they were.

"They did it," he said. "They killed an Alien colony! This place must have been filled with crystals – established. We built a fortification around it then attacked . . . the men fought in . . . they were killed . . . so we flooded the place . . you've seen what water does to Aliens. It won the battle . . ." His voice trailed off, his eyes widened. He sat down. "Unless . . ."

"You OK?" I mean, he was an old man . . . fifty-five or -six. He just looked at me.

"But you see . . . You see what it could mean? Free Men . . . unmodified – lots of them, well-armed – attacking established Aliens? It might be their world! Not ours!"

He seemed to pull himself together and looked about us to see no one was listening.

"It means we're the bloody aggressors . . . the Aliens were victims! Our victims! This was their world!"

"But they said they were space travellers . . . they ruled the galaxy – they said all worlds were theirs by conquest."

"I don't know." Rutherford was hardly listening. "Bluff . . . trying to scare you off . . . even galactic people have to come from somewhere . . ."

"But the ship . . . ?"

"Couldn't it be human . . couldn't it be ours?" He waved off my other questions. He just sat there thinking.

I stood beside him. It's a nasty thing, suddenly finding you might be Alien.

CHAPTER FOURTEEN

PRECIOUS little went on in Craghead's place. Total boredom was the characteristic of the Underground. Boredom and somehow worse than that, a sort of vacuum of inertia . . . a great nothing. It was poisonous.

I mean, those last weeks, plenty had happened – great events . . . meaningful things – and now we had to watch Old Craghead arranging his attributes, trying to jack up his status with the things Old Rutherford had found for him. Nobody cared a damn about what had been done in the south, I had a desperation to go see what that thing was that might be a starship, but I was frightened too – there was hell going on outside.

There were a lot of desperate people raging out there. Man – most of them didn't even have any food now the Aliens were gone . . . worse than that there was no one to tell them what to think. The people just milled about killing each other. Young Craghead's scouts said there was cannibalism on the Border. Those people were struggling back to awareness and finding they were hungry and vicious, that they had nothing after all. Or maybe it was the hunger pangs that were waking them. They found that all the dreams of peace and sunshine and plenty were just figments that the Aliens had plugged into them and then they went mad . . . starving and angry and then insane with it. A man out on the Border wouldn't have lasted five minutes right then, not by himself . . . not on the open Border with nowhere to hide. So I stayed and fumed.

All the same, it ought to have been better than that. It ought to be better than that when men were free. Not only outside too, in a way it was as bad in Craghead's place, humanity was just plain mired in its own villainy and bloody-mindedness, the sickness clung like a black smoke shadow to everyone. I mean, you ought to be able to trust at least some people. There ought to be some pleasantness in the world sometimes.

I mean, was it best to have killed the Aliens and dumped the people on their own devices? Wouldn't they have been better as happy slaves pushing on those waterwheels? Then I thought: "Sure, visions and happiness are OK but what you need is truth. What good are illusions anyway – imaginations and dreams – what good are they to anyone. The small fantasies of small people . . . you only get what's really there, the first thing you want is the truth, then you can go on from that." But all the same it half seemed to me that the Aliens had given more than that . . . and we'd taken away the poor people's happiness and given them their bloody humanity. It didn't seem a fair exchange.

There was a doubt, maybe we'd destroyed something a whole lot more worthy than we'd ever be. Sometimes, looking about me, I was sure we had. I thought and worried at it, wondered scowling through the magnificent palace that Craghead was making for himself on the lower level. I was on the downswing . . . time was slow.

You should have seen what Craghead had there now. He had twelve steps up his dais instead of the old four. The walls were all painted and furbished down there – all those machines that didn't work, all the useless ammunition brought down in great piles for his glory.

Some days I went and found that singing guy I used to listen to before. He'd ask me how it happened up in the crystal Mountains. I'd tell him and feel sad. All the time I was answering he'd be plucking away at that harp of his, those four hands weaving and balancing sweet landscapes of music, then, later maybe, he'd sing that song about snowflakes and melting.

> Slow drift down . . . Or up, in the infinite passage
> Of time of space . . . How can it matter?
> Conquer for brief time . . . Somehow different . . .
> Somehow similar . . . All in the long time . . .
> In space it doesn't matter much.

That song, the stringing and changes he gave it, it seemed to mean something big. Maybe I've got it wrong, but somehow it was like it was all about the Aliens and maybe us too, that spirit that carried them over the galaxy . . . and how it was all the same really. . . . I don't know, I'm no poet. Maybe it was just that it was a man-song and a man was singing it. Anyway, it was comforting.

I mentioned to the music guy about how I wanted to go and see that ship, see whose it was, how it seemed so crucial to me to find out what it was. How what I really cared about now was the early history of the planet. He smiled and said he could understand that. Then he pointed out the danger of things out there.

"Even if you make it," he said, "you've still got to get in . . . anyway – they're dead. No matter how wise they were, they're dead now. You killed them, face it, it's over. It's past grief. The first thing you've got to do is survive." It's easy for artists.

Later I put the same thing to the girl, I didn't mention the ship might be human. She said not to bother her with harebrained, pointless, dangerous schemes, that there was plenty to do here without going looking for trouble. She was busy with Craghead almost all the time, helping him set up his new court. I had the impression she was preoccupied with something else though. Maybe she had a conscience, like me.

Old Rutherford was busy too, working through all the material they'd found when the level was cleared. He'd got it all laid out, weapons and bones related to each other, he was counting them, trying to work out how things must have been. I asked him about leaving it and going out to look at the ship – if that's what it was – but he smiled and shook his head and said not to talk about it.

"That thing out there, it's working on my mind," I said. "We ought to find out . . . it'll tell us. I've *got* to know!"

A deserted thing out there . . . enormous and lying there for God knows how long . . . we *had* to go out and see what it was. Get the answers it must contain.

"You bide your time," said Rutherford. He arranged a mud-stained skull into its attendant helmet. "There . . . it all works out." He stood up. "You see – give it time and it works out." He made a note in a small book he had. "Anyway – how are you going to get in a thing like that? How tough does a starship skin have to be . . . how can you cut into a thing like that?"

"That's what the singer said. A man could find a way . . . there must be a way – a door maybe . . ."

"Singer? You haven't said we thought there was a ship? You haven't told anyone?" I admitted I had. "You damn fool! You know what this place is like Now it's a question if we'll even be allowed to get there!"

I went away before I said something I might regret. I like Old Rutherford – respect him – but he sure asks for it sometimes.

I mean, how dangerous could it be now the Aliens were dead and the Wardens disorganized? Even if it looked like certain death I still thought we should go out there. In a sort of way we owed it to the Aliens.

The next thing that happened – about a week later – was that young Craghead took off to go round the world. He said he was going far south, beyond where the Aliens had been, to see what was what and make contacts for his father. His scouts reckoned that it'd be safe by now, that a lot of those mad people were dead, that it was almost quiet outside.

At first everybody thought it was just another of the enthusiasms young Craghead got – or pretended to get – and that it would soon pass. Nobody thought he'd get more than twenty miles by himself.

When the time came I went up to the surface to watch him set out on his "quest", as he called it. He had about fifty Riders with him, they were loaded down with ropes and provisions, all the tackle they thought they might need. They had three machine guns and a couple of small rockets on packhorses.

When they were all lined up and ready I had to admit they looked good. The horses were pretty fine for a start – all stamping and spirit – and the men had that keen look about them you sometimes see on Mods before they find out what it's all about and start to decay. All the people were watching them and they liked that. All chatter and life out there, all in that early, golden sun.

In the last moment, just as they were moving off that old blue truck that belonged to the girl came whining out of the trees and joined on the back of the column. About then I had one of my bright ideas. I shoved quickly through the crowd and made it out through the main gate. I sure didn't need any girl to show me the way that time. It was an inspiration – sudden – I really felt good about doing something for myself for once, better than for weeks.

The guards weren't even looking as I went out through the maze. There was still some mist about so I must have vanished quite quickly.

I made it down that old road to the south. About two hundred yards down there I sat in a rhododenron, lit a smoke and waited.

It took young Craghead about half an hour to finish getting cheers from the people, but then all the Riders came ringing down the road at a fine canter. It looked great. That column of horses, young Craghead all proud and puffed at the head – they even had a flag.

When they were almost level with me I stepped out and held up my hand. Craghead pulled up his mount and looked down at me. He looked as though he thought something was funny.

"Well, then," he said, "it's Ice Lover. Who'd have thought it? I thought your friends had you well-penned in my father's warren?"

"I want to ride some way south with you," I said. Then, thinking back to how he'd met the girl and me that time: "I must!"

"Ah . . ." He knew what I meant OK. I guess he was wondering how he could take me and still keep all the glory for himself.

"I hope for a friend here as well as behind me," I said. He was looking at my pistol. Maybe he was remembering our first meeting.

"Well then," he said. "Very well. But you shall not have a horse. You must ride the truck – with the other baggage." As he rode past he leaned down and spoke again. "Don't depend so much on friendship, Ice Lover. I have my position now."

I stood back and let the column pass. When the truck showed up I grabbed the windshield and swung myself on board.

It was Rutherford who was driving. I sat down heavily and looked at him. He grinned one of those young grins of his at me and said I looked surprised. I suppose I was, but I should have known that he'd have to go to that ship sooner or later.

"I knew you'd make it," he said. "I knew you'd show up on the way."

"Young Craghead's going to the ship then?"

"Only to leave me with a couple of men. His ride south is genuine enough. Old Craghead doesn't really see any value in going to the ship. Maybe that girl of yours got at him ... she'll sure be wild when she finds we've got her truck!"

There were still people about, a few isolated bands, or hungry-looking men walking by themselves, all that was left of the dispossessed. There were Wardens too, but they only tried to kill you if you were going south or north – east and west they ignored you. Those Alien fragments were still doing their best for the Happy Land. The remaining people were pretty savage. It was amazing how quickly they'd learned.

The Riders got ahead of us in the beech trees. By the time we were on the last fringe before the Border they were a couple of miles ahead. Young Craghead seemed to be trying to hold them back to wait for us, but after a while he couldn't hold them any more and they galloped on and left us.

Half a minute later and we were glad they had. Three

of those moth-shaped flying things like in Craghead's Underground came streaking out of nowhere and laid the whole straggled gaggle of Riders wide open with fire and explosions. One minute they were there and the next they were gone and disappeared into screams and boiling fire and smoke.

Horsemen broke out of the dust in all directions. There were twenty or thirty alive still – it was amazing. A great black balloon of smoke bloomed and towered up there and the Riders breaking from it ... some were still on their horses, then some were running and, later, some were crawling. Each time I saw another survivor I was amazed.

Rutherford swore and swore and reversed the truck back into the thickest bushes he could find. He cut the motor and we dived for cover as the truck settled off its cushion.

On the Border you could still see Riders running. Some made it to the trees. Some hid out in the bare gullies and stones out there. They didn't have a chance because then the hoverers showed up. A dozen maybe. More than I'd ever seen together before ... swimming up from the south in a formation ... like a silver carpet on the sky.

Then the formation broke and they began to quarter the Border, methodically raining down fire and death on anything that lived in the tumbled smoke below.

Old Rutherford and I lay on our bellies and watched the hoverers flitting in and out through the smoke. You could see the Mods in them ... all bloated up in those blue helmets ... firing and shooting their weapons down on the people.

There was a crashing in the bushes on the left, coming towards us. I rolled over and quickly brought up my pistol. I waited.

It was young Craghead. He'd lost his horse and his cloak was on fire. His face was black and his beard full of dust. He came blundering towards us, his mouth opened to speak, or scream, or something. Old Rutherford kicked his legs from under him and he came crashing down beside us.

"Lie still," grated Rutherford. "Lie still and we might get out of it!" Young Craghead lay still and whimpered. He'd lost about everything, he was in shock. He wouldn't be any trouble.

After a while the hoverers had spread out, moved away out of sight as they hunted down the Riders. It was all over, it had taken about five minutes.

Old Rutherford stood up slowly. He looked carefully about. I started to say it looked OK but he cut me off with a gesture. He moved out in the open and stood there, head cocked, listening.

"It's clear," he said. "No sign of them ... can you hear anything?"

"No," I said. I could, but it was very faint. "Let's start – let's get back. The Aliens are still strong someplace. We can make it back!"

We had to push and guide young Craghead into the truck and his knees were knocking. I'd never actually seen a man's knees knocking like that before, he was crying too, but young Craghead always cried awful easy.

Rutherford worked at the controls. We lifted up, shoved through the brambles and into the open. I waited for him to turn north.

He didn't. He kept right on going. South, onto that still dangerous Border.

"You crazy? You crazy old man!" Rutherford just grinned. I don't know if he realized what was happening but young Craghead started to howl.

"We're going to the ship!" Old Rutherford was laughing out loud. "We're going to ride south in that smoke cloud. Like you did before. It's now or never!" He rammed the throttle open and we went screaming south. Craghead was screaming too ... and gibbering. I wasn't feeling so optimistic myself.

We were still in the dust and smoke when we hit the metal plain. At the first edge of it Rutherford brought the truck to a slithering halt in one of the barren gullies there and we piled out. I was surprised to see some grass growing. It didn't seem to be doing much good, but it was trying.

Rutherford was out there stamping on the metal surface, sounding it. That guy! He sure took some chances!

"I'd really like to give it a look-over thoroughly!" he shouted. Shouted mind! In *that* place – on that echoing plain! "It sounds solid here!"

"Keep it quiet" I said. "Please don't shout!"

"Yes . . ." he said. "I don't suppose there's time to survey it . . ."

I was on the metal by now and trying to look over all the horizons at once. There didn't seem to be anything coming. I wondered how long *that* would last. Craghead was sitting in the truck, shivering.

"Yes," said Rutherford. "I guess it'll have to be here." He walked quickly round the truck and opened the back. "Come on then."

We unloaded heavy sacks and cases of explosives onto the metal. When we had about half a ton of old bomb fillings and stuff piled up there Old Rutherford took a remote detonator and shoved it into the boxes and sacks. We spread one of those blast-limiter blankets over the whole thing and Rutherford fused it down with a laser tool. That blanket was there for keeps. Then we repeated the job four times in a semicircle maybe thirty yards across. I kept wishing Craghead would snap out of it and lend a hand.

Rutherford put his hands on his hips and looked at what he had done. He muttered that it'd do.

"The hull can't be *too* thick," he said. "It's a starship – meant for deep space . . . it wouldn't be meant to land – I'm surprised it didn't break up when it got into gravity near a planet . . . all the stress of re-entry. It's down here by accident . . ." He was talking to himself again. I started to worry about Old Rutherford.

We climbed in the truck alongside young Craghead. Rutherford drove off. A mile off we halted.

"Ready?" Rutherford didn't wait for an answer. He yanked the toggle and triggered the explosive.

143

The metal plain seemed to hesitate then heaved up and sounded like a gong.

Fire-tinged black smoke burst up on the curved metal horizon. There was thunder.

"What . . . what the hell was that?" said young Crag-head. Trust him to wake up when all the work was done.

CHAPTER FIFTEEN

WHERE the explosion had been the plain was opened back like one of my sardine cans. There were pale smoke streamers rising there, small flames burned about the place. There were tattered fringes of limiter blanket blowing from the lip of torn metal, there was smoking and flickering there too.

Rutherford brought the truck to a halt and we all got out and looked into the dark hole. It was awesome down there . . . really awesome.

"Sure is dark," said Craghead. It was too. There was a double hull arrangement, the inner one was maybe twelve feet down and deeply corrugated. I couldn't see any connection between the two hulls, I suppose there must have been somewhere.

The inner hull had been damaged too, there were torn holes from metal fragments, you could see an intricate pattern of coloured wiring down there. Some of it was heavy-gauge stuff . . . something to do with being a starship, I guess. The wires were pretty tangled by the explosion, in places the insulation was burning, slowly curling and melting to orange flame and thick smoke.

"Come on," said Rutherford. "We can't wait here! The hoverers'll be back!" He was right. We sure couldn't hang about. There was a breeze blowing up, it ruffled Rutherford's fine hair and the thin-stretched flying-wing fragments of blanket. The smoke from the explosion began to drift away . . . the wind was blowing us no good . . . it was time to go. I leaned forward and peered into the dark. The longer we waited the more dangerous it got.

Rutherford went to the truck. When he came back he had a rope and a tool bag. He tied the bag to the rope and threw it down onto the inner hull. I looked back and saw he'd tied the other end to the lug on the front of the truck.

"Come on," he said. "For God's sake come *on!*" The old fool was over the edge and sliding into the dark. Craghead and I still didn't believe it. We looked at each other and back the way we'd come. Rutherford was across the inner hull and lowering himself through a hole in that. He kept telling us to hurry up.

We were still thinking about maybe making a run for it. Well – I like Rutherford sure, but hell – there are limits. Then we saw the silver glint of hoverers against the distant sky – and they were coming *fast*.

A jump and a slither and I landed sprawled on Craghead on the inner hull. We sorted ourselves out and made for the hole into the ship proper.

We bundled into a corridor down there. It was big, maybe eight feet deep, about twice as wide. In one direction it sloped down, the other way it ran up.

Rutherford was waiting for us. He was enjoying it. He led the way, running hard down the hill. It seemed like a good idea at the time, you can run faster downhill, we just wanted to be away from the pool of daylight under the hole behind us.

At first it all seemed dark, but after a while – when we got away from the hole – we began to see small lights set flush in the corridor floor. When you got used to it you could even see by them.

We must have run about two hundred yards altogether. There wasn't much there, only that grey, dark corridor sloping away from us. We could only see about thirty feet in those lights.

Suddenly the floor was moving steeper and steeper down and we were running more and more downhill – then faster and faster until our legs ran away with us and we couldn't stop.

I don't know what happened to the rest but I flung flat and tried to stop falling. It was no good.

I heard a yell from Rutherford ahead. Then a loud splash. The next second I plunged deep in icy water next to him.

146

Cold ... colder than all the north ... dark and cold, the very centre of coldness and blackness. Someone grabbed my collar and I coughed and spluttered as he dragged me to the edge of the water.

"You OK?" said young Craghead. "You haven't lost your gun?" He was hanging onto the ledge there, onto a lip, the floor of a tunnel about three feet square. There were lights in it, but not as many as before. You could see them leading away and after a while they doubled up, reflected in water. Then they came down and disappeared beneath the surface.

We lay in the cold water looking away down that uninviting tunnel. Then I started getting scared about things that might be swimming about beneath my feet. I jack-knifed and convulsed myself up and out into the tunnel. I reached back and dragged out Old Rutherford. Young Craghead made it himself. Water went cascading from our clothes, it was deafening in that closed space.

The floor wasn't flat like in the corridor. There was all sorts of stuff in it, rails maybe, a little like in the shaft at the Underground but smaller, of course. There were tubes too, scores of them. set in recesses, all looped and striped in varied colours. There were wires as well, they'd been neatly clamped and channelled together once, you could see places where they still were, but mostly they were tangled and confused, hanging and ravelled there, rotting away down that cramped tunnel.

About ten feet down there our feet began to be in water and there was a circular grid set in the ceiling. Rutherford turned when he'd passed it. His face came very near mine, we were doubled right up there, it was murder.

"We have to go up," he said. "We might be able to make it that way ... up here. The grid's not too strong." He got a lever out of his bag and had the grid off in seconds. It felt like plastic of some kind. He stood up into the small shaft behind it, he tied one end of his shortened rope to his tool bag and the other to his belt. He called us to follow and led off up into the hole.

It was a struggle, but in the end we were all in the shaft, our packs hanging behind us, our feet and backs wedged between the walls. There was a nasty corner every thirty feet or so, and junctions that led off to God knows where, but on the whole it wasn't much of a trick to get up there. Rutherford led and he kept going up – ignored any forks that went down and kept going. Craghead's pack kept hitting me about the head, but I fell back a little and then it was all right.

After what seemed like about six hours the shaft seemed to have turned back to horizontal and we discovered we were crawling on our hands and knees. My back was breaking, it was torture.

Then the tunnel came to an end. It widened, then there was a big centrifugal fan thing set there and we couldn't go any further. Rutherford gave a shout of delight.

"Ventilation!" He turned to me. "Still think it's an Alien ship?"

"My father could use one of them," said young Craghead. He meant the fan.

We doubled down a side tube, away from where the fan was. Rutherford kicked out another of the grid things and we scrambled through onto the floor of a new corridor. The lights were brighter, or maybe we were getting used to them, you could see the floor curving away by the way the lights dropped out of sight. There's nothing more unnatural than having the light source beneath you ... almost like being back in the crystal Mountains it was.

"If you're so sure it's a human ship why aren't the lights right?" I said. "Those vents don't have to be for air. And what are those doing there?" I'd just seen a drift of those Alien shell cases over against one of the walls.

Rutherford grunted and led off up the corridor. About then we started hearing noises behind us.

It wasn't anything you could identify. Banging about, footsteps maybe, it was all confused and far away with

148

echoes, you couldn't guess about it. We remembered those hoverers we'd seen and moved on quickly.

All the time we hurried down into the deeps of the ship. There were stairs maybe and ladders most of the way but there were places where they'd broken and then we'd have to spend time looking for the way on. One thing we all felt certain about was that truth lived at the bottom of *this* well – or some of it – and the further we went the further we were from whatever it was behind us.

It was like a maze. Like those fortifications in front of Craghead's enclosure but in three dimensions and complex, it was practically dark at times too, and that didn't help. We lost track of time, judging from my belly it must have been most of a day before we hit the damaged areas.

We were getting near the centre of the ship by then. If you stayed in the parts of the corridors where you could stand and kept going down, then I guess you had to find the centre. Maybe we weren't really lost at all in that case, but it sure felt like it. Anyway, the first time we noticed the damage was when the ladders got to be bent – like they were bowed ... too long for where they were.

Then the walls started to be buckled and it seemed like each corridor was a little lower. There was about a hundred feet of ladder between each corridor, we lost count of ladders. We couldn't find what was between the corridors. There were big doors, but they were shut and we couldn't move them.

At first Rutherford thought there had been some sort of explosion, but as we got on there wasn't any sign of burning or blast. Our footsteps sounded different down there, like there was a tension in the fabric of the place.

Then some of the big doors had sprung open a bit and a couple of corridors below that there were some that were burst right out. We looked in some of them, but there wasn't a lot to see.

There were no lights in there for one thing, mostly

there were just smaller corridors in there and more locked doors. Anything that had been there was spilled and tumbled on the floors. That was how most of the lights had gone, smashed or else they were covered with rubbish. We saw some bones there, but I didn't notice any carapaces or weapons. Then the noises behind us were getting louder, so we had to move on.

Lower still there were carpets of those Alien shells. I asked Rutherford what he made of *that*, but he wouldn't say anything.

Then there were no more ladders. The last had been like a corkscrew so maybe it was as well. We'd come to the final floor.

We had to drop the last ten feet, maybe it was a lot taller at some time. There were all sorts of machinery and screens, knobs and switches, pillars and things like that on metal benches forced and bent onto the floor. The corridor was on a shorter radius – we were near the centre of the ship – but the width of it seemed to stretch away forever, it was more of a room than a corridor down there. It still wasn't brightly lit, but there seemed a lot more power than above.

A bit to the right the ceiling was crushed right down into the floor. Craghead said maybe we could climb round the curve there on the screens and things and so to a corridor further down. After a while the noises behind got louder so we had to try it.

We'd got about halfway round when it hit me. There was a dial right in front of my nose and it registered zero. I could read it! I told Rutherford and he laughed.

"I told you," he said. "It's a man-ship!"

"It's a crazy one. It's not right."

"Haven't you figured that? It's not crazy. It's upside-down ... or partly. The lights are in the floor because that's the ceiling. Some sort of centrifugal gravity ... made to spin. The thing is collapsing under its own weight too ... as I said, it was made for deep space – it's on the surface by accident."

Right then we had an interruption. Craghead had been climbing on while we were talking. He suddenly yelled there was something up front, something moving.

I hung out on one hand and tried to get my pistol free with the other. There was a rustle ahead and something scurried away from us.

We went after it and a few minutes later we had our feet on something that really was a floor.

It was wonderful to have lights overhead again. Now we were past the ship's dead centre other things were right too. Like those scored pads were on top of the ladder rungs now ... it was a great comfort, things were a lot more natural.

Then this guy came out of the shadows.

"Strangers," he said. "Have you come from above ... is the air good ... oxygen ... is there Pink?" He was armed, there was a big pistol on his hip but he didn't make any move for it, so I didn't shoot him. He looked pale – a little dazed – but OK. His uniform was neat.

"Ah," he said. "Is it time then? Have we made planet fall? Is this the coming and the revelation?" He wiped his hand over his eyes. "Are you our rescuers then? If you are ours there should be more. Where are the rest? Are there only three of us left ... four?" He spoke Free talk, but he used some funny words – sometimes it sounded wrong, but you could tell what he meant.

"The rest?" said Rutherford. "What do you think has happened?"

Craghead was looking at us. He came forward. He was waving his gun about.

"God damn it!" he said. "That's Free Man's talk! You're Free Men! I thought there was something funny about you!" The pale guy turned when Craghead spoke. I guess he saw him for the first time.

"ALIEN! God – it's horrible!" I never saw a man look more shocked. Mind, when you really looked at Craghead he was something to scare kids with. I mean, that skin and those tufts of hair ... that pared-back carapace! That poor guy wasn't prepared like you and me.

151

The pale guy clawed at the pistol on his belt. Craghead shot him. It was all over so quickly. There wasn't time to do anything. Craghead glared at us through the smoke.

"Now then," he said. *"Free Men!"* That carapace of his up against the light ... it looked like the translucent body on a housefly.

"Put it away," said Rutherford. "You can trust us ... surely after all this time ...?"

We ignored Craghead's gun and stooped over the pale guy. Craghead hadn't killed him properly but he was going down fast.

"Aliens," he said after a while. "Aliens on the ship ...?" He sounded just mildly anxious, the guy was dying. I don't think he was in any pain, he was long past that. "And the damage too ... all the damage.... Everybody's dead you know. ... We found a new world – green it was, nice – suitable, compatible ... so we settled a colony, all the plants and trees from the ship ... cows and farming, then we came back to earth ... orders to return ... but something went wrong. We entered the atmosphere ... crashed, came down ... settled breaking into an inland sea ... and then there was the Pink ... all wrong. The ship is collapsing and there's Pink all around and we can't get out ... so we went into preservation – like in space – set a superlight barrier – the ship is wrecked and there's Pink all about us ... and everybody dead ... and all the armies are defeated ... and the Aliens gather ..." He died then.

Rutherford reckoned that it was as much that he was too quick out of this "preservation" – whatever that was exactly – as Craghead's bullet. He died easy though, relaxed, not fighting in vain to live. I guess his agony was over a long time before.

We couldn't get everywhere down there but we looked where we could. The lower you went the more crushed things were. A corridor or two down and there was water again, I guess the whole ship was like a sump for the surrounding country. Maybe the water was that inland sea the pale guy was speaking of.

We found other guys there, the rest of the crew, I guess, or some of them. Pathetic bird's nests of bones all hanging and tangled in the preservation machines.

In places there were great depths of the Alien shells too, so they'd been there as well. God knows how they got in, or what they did, or what killed them. How the pale guy had survived I couldn't guess either. Maybe it had been flooded where he was, or maybe he had special protection in some way. What happened to him sure wasn't worth getting up for though!

It was a sad thought. There was an epic sadness about it. This ancient agony. Those men, guarding and transporting those Colonists through all those aeons and light-years across the galaxy. Fulfilling that, finding them their paradise, their new star, their new world ... then starting back, starting home at the time of the Defeat ... and finding humanity there perverted and modified by the Pink ... the world ruined and destroyed. Finding there was nothing they could do about it. Then preservation and dying in despair and far from light. I wish I knew that pale guy's name, maybe I could have scratched it on a wall or something.

CHAPTER SIXTEEN

I SAID we took a look around down there but there wasn't really much to see. We had plenty of trouble just getting about. Mostly there was only one passable way and the rest was a chaos of twisted metál, the walls all concertinaed and the passage like a dog's hind-leg. In places the ceilings had come down in great sheets, the walls had buckled and the lights that were working staggered crazy away in the twisted and confined space. Mostly there was only about three feet to move in, it was really hard going.

There were noises behind us again. You couldn't really be certain. For one thing the whole structure seemed to be alive and moaning – clicking with the enormous weight above – but every so often we were sure we heard something. One thing, it couldn't be the pale guy any more ... something had to be following us ... we drove deeper and deeper, we sure didn't want to hang about down there.

Then everything was flattened and sealed tight and there were pools of water to show how it flooded sometimes. We got about fifty yards another way, down the slope and then we hit deep water. There was no way of going on.

We went back and stood under the crooked way we'd come down. We had to climb back up there towards the noises, there was only one way to go. No one wanted to be first.

In the end I got to thinking how it might rain and how if it did we'd soon be under water, so I poked my pistol first and began to climb. The others followed and sometimes I stopped to listen, but all I could hear was Old Rutherford breathing and the tension of the ship. The buckled shaft was too uncomfortable to wait in long so I soon gave up and moved on.

I made an effort and brought my eyes to floor level. I eased my pistol up and looked out over the floor. It was waved like the sea. I remember thinking the ship would crush us yet and save the bother of climbing up. Then I saw a movement over the pale guy's body. I swung the pistol.

"No! Don't shoot! It's me!" The girl stood up and waved frantically. I was so surprised I nearly shot her anyway.

We straggled up the ladder and onto the distorted floor. We stared at the girl in the funny half-light. She was alone, her and her four breasts, it was amazing. I wouldn't have gone into the ship by myself, not for anything.

"I was following you," she said. "I saw you take my truck, of course I followed."

"What about the hoverers?"

"You know you can dodge them when you're by yourself. There was still a lot of smoke from your blasting anyway." We stood quiet, then Craghead moved over beside her.

"Them ... they're *Free Men!*" he said. "We Mods – we've got to stick together. . . . I heard them talking Free talk!"

"Ah ..." said the girl. "Now that explains a lot ... the question is, does it change things?" She didn't seem very surprised but you couldn't tell in that light. It didn't seem she'd make a fuss ... I wondered what she would do.

"Right now we've got to get out of here," said Rutherford. There was cracking and creaking all around us, it was getting on his nerves too. I suppose the ship had been there a long time – if it was going to collapse it would have by now – but then all I wanted was out.

"No," said the girl. "We mustn't fight. We're all human." So we were – basically.

There wasn't much talking on the way up. Once we'd got round the centre it was easy. Almost a whole day's climbing and we were out. I was aching in every joint.

155

It was raining again up there. There wasn't any sign of the hoverers, they never seem to hang about for long. We quickly climbed aboard the truck and the girl drove off.

Now he'd had a day to get used to the idea, Craghead seemed to have accepted us again – forgotten we were Free Men. He was quieter than usual, but it was almost like old times. He was like that, his moods were violent but they soon burned out. The girl taking the news so easy threw him a bit too. But we were all human – you couldn't deny it – we had to get together and rebuild earth like it was ... it was no good to fight amongst ourselves.

It kept on raining all the way to the Underground.

The refugees had all gone by the time we got back there. Gone back to their farming and the need to make a living, you can't leave farming for long. Old Rutherford thought it ought to be a good year as long as nothing went wrong. Some of the Alien things were still working, some Wardens for example ... and those hoverers. But he reckoned all the Aliens were dead and that things would soon be back to normal.

Craghead went off as soon as we got back. He muttered something about getting off on another quest – he said he wasn't going near the ship this time. I watched him disappear through the crowd. I didn't trust him or his Mods, it struck me how I should have put a bullet in him and the girl before they had a chance to talk about Rutherford and me. I wasn't sorry we hadn't though. I thought how I must be getting soft.

We hadn't got into the Underground barely ten minutes when someone came yelling for Rutherford. We followed the excited Mod to the bottom of the shaft. On the way he shouted back through the steam and noise of the engines what had happened.

They'd found another level. A third one. Below Craghead's new place.

There'd been nothing to suggest it was there – when

156

Rutherford left to go to the ship he told his men to keep working and pumping at the bottom of the shaft. To keep it dry as much as anything, he said.

After about a day they hit bottom. There'd been a load of machinery there, tangled cables and winches, a couple of wrecked hoverers, stuff like that and the usual bones and Alien shells, before they hit plastic.

Rutherford wasn't there to stop them, so they kept on going down. They softened the plastic with fire and hauled it, burning and smoking, up the shaft. Then, because Rutherford still wasn't back, they started on the concrete. First they used picks, then, when that was too slow, they blasted.

There was about ten feet of concrete and when they got through that there was limestone. They kept on going. They blew the last charge and it was like knocking the keystone out of an arch. The whole thing fell through into the cave beneath. They said there was a hell of a splash. They'd been sitting there ever since pointing guns into the dark.

Rutherford talked to them and after a while persuaded them that there was no danger.

I moved into the shadows where I could see everything. We hadn't seen the girl for a while and I didn't know if young Craghead was trying to pull anything. Someone had to look out – Rutherford seemed to have forgotten everything in his excitement.

I don't know what he expected to find down there but he was like a little boy with it. He used to say a man's problem was to find a problem, if you had a problem and you were thinking then you were OK.

It was an uneasy time though. Waiting there in the guttering light and steamy air, amongst those falling ashes and the naked, sweating Mods. Waiting for Craghead or the girl to get at us . . . and all the time the brooding blackness of that cave beneath . . . that *void* there. I kept thinking about flies and wishing I was in the north.

In the end Rutherford found a sucker with infra-red vision and lowered him down there on the end of a rope.

As he went he yelled it was a river down there, not very fast and that he could see the shores. We lowered him on down and heard him splash in the water. A little later he yelled again and said the shore was firm enough and there were good places to fix ropes. Two hours later and they had a rope and timber bridge down to the floor of the cave so we wouldn't get our feet wet

It was a nervous business going down that bridge. The first hundred feet were more or less vertical, then it levelled off and the last part was up again. It was cold down there, damp, you could hardly hear anything for the sound of water falling. Rutherford had men spreading all over the cave with torches so we could see what sort of place it was.

The river was really quite big. About fifty feet across, set right in the floor of the cave, there were places like it had been bigger once and cut other ways further up. As the torches moved you could see the whole place was filled with what Rutherford called stalagmites and stalactites, some of them were enormous. I didn't like it much, it was like being inside that crystal Mountain again – except it was cool and mysterious. That constant plopping of water from maybe two hundred feet above didn't help either. It didn't seem to worry the Mods though, there's nothing that worries Mods, they're stupid ... They should have been worried ... I stuck close to Rutherford.

As those guys explored down the cave, showed it to us with their torches, it slowly dawned just how big it was. It was so clean too, all that washed sand, those polished pebbles ... it was so moist and clean and sweet. There wasn't a spot of rubbish anywhere. It was so untouched – virgin – like a cathedral of hygiene. It was strange to walk where maybe no one else had ever been.

Far up the cave we got a bit ahead of the Mods and came to a great slab of limestone lying where it had fallen from the roof. There were water ripples worn on

it, I remember a stumpy stalagmite growing on top . . .
it was perfect, white as linen.

Then, suddenly, our torches lit a pattern of oval pools
cut deep in it. When we looked there were white fish in
them with no eyes. They seemed to sense the light
though and huddled deep in the water. They were horrible.

"But the pools are the thing," said Rutherford.
"They're cut perfect. Who made them to keep their fish
fresh . . .? Maybe they're ancient and the fish acciden-
tal . . ."

"Are you . . . men?" said someone in the darkness.
"Are you from the Great Light Above Ground? Those
promised to relieve our gloom?"

"My God!" said Rutherford. "Mods!"

There were maybe six of them – or sixty – we couldn't
tell. We couldn't see . . . but they could sure see us.

Rutherford held up his torch and lunged forward. I
had my hand on my pistol, but I kept it under my
clothes. I couldn't see what we were up against, it's not
a bit of good flashing your weapon out if you don't
know what you're going to do with it.

They were briefly in the light, then they moved back.
They said it hurt their eyes – to keep it away. Those
eyes . . . the damnedest great things you ever saw!

They were magnificent. Forget about those tatty Mods
you see every day. I never saw Mods like these were.
They were taller than me, their pelts were gold and
brown and shining. The carapaces were splendid . . .
they had them set about with blue stones and inlaid
gold. They had short swords and they had gold-studded
rifles too. Their eyes were big and deep and lapis and
violet. I glimpsed their secondary arms neatly tucked
against their chests. The bare parts were white, like perfect plastic, like driven snow. They were magnificent,
you could feel them pity us in our dirty furs and in-
complete bodies. They were magnificent.

"You must come with us," said the boss one. "Do
not call for your servants."

When they realized we couldn't see like them they had

us put our hands on their shoulders and led us off into the dark like blind men. I didn't like that much either, but you couldn't argue, we had to go. I kept my other hand on my pistol – maybe there'd be another chance later.

Altogether I think we must have walked about ten miles. A lot of the time it was up and down, or in winding passages, so I don't suppose we finished more than maybe five from where we started.

Those narrow passages, twisting and lumping in on us, sometimes knee-deep in running water, they went on forever. There was the sound of water everywhere, falling and dripping, sounding and booming in the wet infinity of the caverns. There were places where they actually had to pull us through, sometimes you had to strip before you moved on, then lie still, not struggle, then push your greased body through with tiny movements of your fingers and toes. Those walls fitted you like your skin. I kept thinking about how there might be an earth tremor and how the rock only need move a half inch and I'd be there forever.

There were big places too. Enormous volumes where only remote echoes said how big they were. Then, in the bigger caves, there were lights. At first I thought they were only phosphorescence, but then I saw they were artificial. They looked like those old lights, the sort that go forever if you keep them low.

Then there were what you'd have to call gardens. Hydroponics, Rutherford whispered – they probably were too, they weren't any sort of plant I recognized. They were pale yellow-green and gold, there were women working there – Breeders, I mean – and children with them. We saw maybe two hundred people on that trip, but that would only be part of it, you couldn't tell how many there might be.

At the end of a wider passage with plants growing in the white, sand floor we came to where they lived. We still couldn't see much. There was only the dim glow of the old lamps and that was meant for the plants – they didn't seem to need much.

160

There was muttering up ahead. It was Mod talk and we could understand what we heard of it, it didn't use any Free talk at all, so it wasn't easy. Not that they were trying to hide anything from us, and they never hurt us either. I liked them, they were gentle. Then a small, still voice spoke up and ordered us brought forward and that there should be light, so that we could see. Then there was light, but not much.

They were standing there, looking at us with their violet eyes. Scores of them, women and kids too. White like those fish, white against the glory of those lustrous pelts.

Right in front of us, on a dais like Craghead's, there were sixteen or eighteen little guys. They had pale fur, their faces and arms were the same bone-white. They were exactly like the others except you couldn't tell exactly how many there were because they only had one carapace between them.

It was the worst thing I think I've ever seen. That carapace ... it was like a bunch of flat grapes. There were some faces you could see on the outside ... they were like dolls' ... all the eyes that could were swivelled to look at us. Sharp little things ... like old babies' ... sharp and not moving.

Inside the heads merged – well, connected anyway – you couldn't really see, thank God. The arms and legs that were visible were so thin ... like a fly's, but white ... you could see dark veins lying under the flesh.

The whole thing moved towards us. Those little legs were crammed so close together that they could only take tiny steps. They couldn't have moved about much. I didn't blame them for living down in the dark ... you wouldn't have gone out much if you looked like that. The Aliens sure had a lot to answer for, I hated them all over again, even if they were dead. The nearest face opened its mouth and started talking. The rest still looked at us ... all the time they hadn't blinked once. The faces that weren't talking just pursed their little prune mouths.

161

"We have come from our soft place so that you can see us. It is an honour. You may thank us."

"Thank you," said Rutherford. He was more worried than I'd ever seen him. He was death-pale ... maybe it was the light – all that effort through the passages, his mouth was a little open.

"You have come to signify that it is safe to walk in the On-the-Surface? That the evil Pink is dead and gone? That we can come again In-the-Light with safety?"

"The Alien has gone," said Rutherford. "My friend, this man, has killed it." For a moment all those chilling little eyes switched at me.

"For that, thank you. However, it is a small thing. It was weakened – a few more years and we would have killed it ourselves. In any event we had avoided it by entering the caves. Our origins were here – we have long escaped back here from predators. Our carapaces are an adaptation to protect tender brains from bumpy roofs. We have made our domain here again ... we have re-adapted. You have no carapaces?

"We must reclaim. We Brain Modified must lead our people to their own. We thank you that you have made it possible."

"Modified," said Rutherford. "Please explain that to me. I am old ... I merely desire to know. Why did the Pink Alien modify men for wisdom?"

"You must understand that by now? You must understand that we are not men? That this is our world and men were Aliens too? That you are not pure – but tainted by manhood?

"That first men and then the Pink took this world – or parts of it – from us, the true people?" I didn't say a word, neither did Rutherford. It was all clicking into place. I was numb, shocked.

"The man-race was hard on us – they took our surface, raped it with their plants and trees ... to some extent perverted its atmosphere ... farmed our lands ... hunted us with science and weapons we did not un-

162

derstand. Built fortresses on our entry places . . . formed
our upper galleries to their rule of right angle . . . con-
demned us to the under world they could not use or
hunt us through . . . filled the planet with death things.
Took our brothers for servants, saying they were too
foolish for other things, nobler things. We hold much
against men."

"But we kept our deep home!" Another head took
up the speech. "We lived and thrived pure here . . . per-
ferring darkness for our nocturnal eyes and ears. We have
survived pure from the genetic chaos above.

"Early on our fathers decided that to survive we must
be like men. Combine . . . learn the things we could not
master . . . the conquest drive we lacked and needed . . .
combine that some of our people might some day have
some of their rights.

"Always our race had the property of quick and easy
change and evolution . . . the almost conscious modification of our bodies from one generation to the next.
Some of our people were changed to be more like men –
to breed with them – we made that modification to
gather to our race men's genes and intelligence. It was
no great thing. The chance and profusion of the uni-
verse had made an almost parallel evolution . . . it had
to be somewhere, it was of our races. There were simi-
larities and differences . . . our two races were not dis-
parate.

"Our females were more fertile than man's – we
would not lose by biological combination – we made
them more so. Nobody would lose . . . it was a fair settlement.

"Men prospered . . . the new race grew. The man-ship
saw all was well, it could do no more, it left orbit and
turned for home. All looked well . . . and the Pink Alien
came.

"Undetected – seeding in – a thousand small crystal
ships . . . and we . . . we joined it as an ally . . .

"We hated men enough for that in those days. It
seemed ideal . . . its skills were ours . . . biological . . . it

163

almost seemed more like us. Perhaps we thought we could live with it and still keep our racial identity. But the Pink turned and subjugated us also when all the men were dead. All tumbled down in ruin ... we were more servile than ever. ...

"The Pink plucked back the man-ship from superlight ... dashed it down. The Pink was skilled in such things. No help would come for men ... how will men find this world again? We are safe.

"The foul Pink found us easy to work with ... a new and sympathetic material ... our easy evolution ... our modification ... that made the chaos above ... the man-combinations and impurities of which you are the product ... the bastard race of crazy crossbreeding ... the people you call Mods ... they are not our people ... perhaps they are close ... perhaps there will be a place for them. ...

"But our pure Originals ... we will rule the world. If the man-bastards know their place we will be merciful ... there will be some small station for them in our new order."

"From underground?" said Rutherford. "How can a few cave dwellers conquer a world? How are you going to take on a tough thug like Craghead?" He didn't say anything about us being Free Men. He didn't say anything about Free Men at all. I guess there were so few of us they'd not noticed. Rutherford wasn't stupid enough to mention it.

Anyway it hadn't changed. Being a Free Man was going to be something you didn't shout about ... like always. I kept wishing we'd put a bullet in young Craghead and the girl. Maybe it still wasn't too late.

"This limestone mass is half the continent," said the Think Mod. "There are millions of these caves, all connected now, we have them all. There are enough of us, enough for an elite – which is what matters.

"We tell you this for you have killed the Alien Pink. We have heard you have done great things in Craghead's Underground. For this – even though you have man-blood ... no carapaces ... and are bastards – we

164

will honour you. We will need Mods of determination to help us rule the world ... there is hope even if you have no carapace ..."

For the time it looked as if we might be OK, I just had to get at young Craghead and the girl .. with them dead we could relax. These Originals sure did care about carapaces ... if I killed those two Mods, Rutherford and me might even last a month.

CHAPTER SEVENTEEN

So we were taken back to the surface. They didn't try to disarm us or anything. They were polite and considerate but you always had the feeling there was a big Original standing near for if we made any sudden moves. What could we do anyway, in that dark, against guys with eyes like theirs? Really I suppose they mostly ignored us as irrelevant and beneath their interest. I got angry about that.

That cave system of theirs made Craghead's look like a mousehole. The Originals proudly told us of the riddled complexity of the caves and water passages. We saw animals too, funny indigenous things like pretty little else. The Originals said they milked a kind of bat they had, but I don't know if they were joking.

Rutherford reckoned that maybe the planet was liable to recurring ice ages, that the people were driven out of the caves by flood water when the ice melted, then had to go back again when it got cold and the water was locked up in ice again. He said that would be why the caves were so big and extensive – all that repeating melting ice water, and that was why the Originals were so adapted for cave life.

Old Craghead was suspicious at first – he soon got over that and then he went mad with enthusiasm. He took those splendid Originals as a vindication of himself personally. It was pathetic to watch him run round after them. He made Originals stand near him and glowed with reflected glory. He'd keep glancing up at them to make sure it wasn't all a dream.

I had to admit they looked pretty good, all healthy and noble amongst the ragtag of Craghead's Underground. They looked about them with a sort of horror at the human characteristics mixed up in the Mods, at the way they behaved. You know, like the guys with only two arms – and those who'd cut off their secondaries to be like men ... the Breeders that hadn't got all they should have. The Originals were particularly shocked by the Mods who'd pared back their carapaces so there was just a fragment left on the crowns of their heads, then stained it so it looked like hair. It wasn't so bad for those guys in a way. I mean a carapace will grow again.

The Mods were really arrogant now. They strutted and preened themselves, pretending to know big words and to think deeply. They even tried to shove Old Rutherford and me about, but the Originals wouldn't let them do anything really bad, so mostly we were ignored. I felt like a ghost.

Then Craghead moved up onto the surface. Shifted his whole court up there, said the world belonged to his people and by God he was going to have it.

Those Brain Modified Originals told him how the big doors opened and the ramps dropped down and Craghead had his attributes brought up. He had a couple of the flying machines there, he used to sit behind the discoloured glass up front of one and pretend he was God. Just sat up there, his chin on one hand, glaring down on the people. He had a big board and vellum set up and he'd spend his days drawing up plans of what he might do one day when he got to it. It was pathetic, but you had to admit he had the art of ruling down pat – he knew that as a ruler he must do nothing and so make no mistakes.

In the end the whole of the Enclosure, all the open space up there, was scattered with weapons and machinery he'd brought up. Great piles of ammunition and rockets for everyone to help themselves. Then he wondered why there was hardly any left at the end of the week.

The Originals set up in the cave, by the way, the one with the fish tanks. I believe they brought the Brain Modified that far, they liked to be where they controlled things. Old Craghead turned out to be so slavish taking orders I guess they decided to use him for a while.

167

It was sickening how the Mods pretended to be Originals, that the light hurt them and so on. They let their carapaces grow down over their eyes like goggles and Craghead had a wooden frame built all over the entry shaft and his flying machines and the whole thing covered with fabric and tarred. It was like that thing the Charcoal Burner had all that time ago, but enormous; Craghead had a lot of trouble keeping his thin blood warm in there. For a while they all tried to live in the dark, but they soon gave that game up and cut windows.

They went in for pageants and banners too, hanging blue stones on their carapaces. Craghead's new aristocracy of Originals looked on and tried to bend things to some sort of sensible order and administration. Sometimes I saw them smiling amongst themselves. There'd be a sorting out one day – the chaff would burn then.

One day I was sitting on Rutherford's square pipes watching the water and worrying about the old guy. He was going down fast, letting himself slip into a cringing depression. Craghead seemed to enjoy watching him, but I hated to see him go like that. He was the only thing that kept me there really, a sort of loyalty to the poor old guy. I suppose it happens to us all in the end, old age I mean.

Anyway, I was sitting there in the sun thinking about making a break for the north, when I saw the girl coming towards me.

She was high in the new setup. The Originals liked her – they always respected intelligence – and she was something to see.

She wore a tabard of cloth of gold and a white shift thing with blue decoration underneath. She'd cut her hair like an Original Breeder and her face was painted the correct dead white. She had fur underneath to make up for the pelt she didn't have.

"Well, Ice Lover ... Free Man," she said. "Is the great man deserted now? Don't they love you for your pistol any more?"

I scowled at her and said I was going north. She kept

looking over my head. Couldn't face me I thought, after we'd been through so much together. There were people about, I didn't have anything to say.

"No, don't go north," she said. "It won't always be like this." I nodded, I'd go north all right, when I was ready.

"They'll need good men one day..." she met my eyes, saw what I was thinking. Her eyes went down, she stirred the grass with her foot. "Very well then, come with me. There's something I must show you."

We walked all across the Enclosure, far away from Craghead's tarred palace. She didn't say much, we just walked on over and through the summer grass and wild flowers. I was thinking that if we got somewhere really quiet I might put my knife in her and that'd be one less that knew I was a Free Man.

When we had walked maybe fifteen minutes she turned and looked back across the drifting grass dust to where Craghead's place looked like one of those card castles that people make. There was no one out in the midday sun, they were all inside pretending to be blinded by the heat.

"This'll do," she said. She struck off into the dark cool of some chestnut trees there. She twitched off her sun visor and looked at me. "Yes ... I can see you now ... we must stay here awhile ... I'll show you so you can trust me ..."

She lifted the tabard over her head, then wiped the paint off her face. She turned from me and I saw by her movements she was unfastening her tunic. She let that drop and unstrung the fine furs that were beneath it. Her back was pale and beautiful in the green light. It was crossed with thin, white straps.

"What – you give up that drug?" It was all I could think of to say. She was a Mod, but right then I wanted her. Even the grossest Breeders had ignored me since the Originals came. When you stop getting a thing that's when you really want it.

She turned. She reached behind her back. Her breasts had a sort of four-cupped garment. Maybe that was why

169

she always looked so young and didn't slop about the way most Breeders did.

She unfastened whatever it was behind her and the last garment came off. The lower breasts came with it.

She was a Free Man ... Woman. She smiled.

"You see ... I'm human ... I don't need drugs."

I held out my arms and she came and burrowed her nakedness into my furs. She was thin really ... a lithe creature. She was a real human and I loved her.

There was a sound of thunder, a rumble very distant. I thought it was in my head, but the girl twisted away from me.

"No," she said. "Not now. There isn't time." She broke away, caught up her clothes and pulled them on as she went to the edge of the trees. She pulled something out of her furs and started talking into it, all the time peering anxiously to the west. I noticed she'd left off the extra breasts. She hadn't put on her fur things either.

Out of the west there was a shriek and a roar. Orange and black fire erupted around the shaft. Craghead's playing-card palace dissolved in flying planks and splashing earth. The tent part billowed into the air then burned like a wisp of tinder. It was Armageddon. I lay close to the girl and we watched it all.

There was a moment's silence. I noticed the birds had stopped singing and there were people screaming. Then there was another series of explosions.

The people and the palace were torn to bits. Again and again fire thundered over that part of the Enclosure. When it had stopped there was only blackened earth and curling smoke a thousand feet in the air. In the new silence there were fewer screams.

"We want the shaft," said the girl. "You come on. The shaft is the only entry we're sure of." She broke off to speak in that thing of hers. "Come on! I need you. We've got to get to those explosives in the Underground. We mustn't let them blow the shaft!"

We started to run through the grass to where the burning had been. I wanted to ask her what was happening,

170

but I couldn't find the breath. The birds had started singing again, or some of them.

At the shaft there were burned Mods everywhere. Black, charred and stinking. On the outskirts some were still alive, wondering and weeping and dazed. When they came too close the girl shot them with that little pistol of hers. Explosive bullets sure do spread a man out.

The dead and dying were thickest near the shaft entrance. It seemed everybody had tried to make it there when the explosions started. The parapet round the shaft was splintered with the heat, fresh splintered stone showed amongst the blackening. The iron work was still hot, you couldn't touch it.

There was a carpet of blackened corpses to walk on. I'll remember that forever. Those bodies half burned ... crusted outside and the smell of cooking as our feet broke through.

In the shaft it was really unbearable. The rungs struck hot through your boot soles and at first the uprights were burning. The girl had heavy gloves and I used my gauntlets from the ice. I thought I'd melt inside my furs so I got rid of most of them. Concealment didn't seem to matter any more. The grease in my pistol started to melt and made my gauntlets slippery. By the time I got twenty feet down the shaft my hands and belly were blistered but I'd stopped caring by then.

There were still people alive in the treadmill and lying around on the grid. I guess they got nearly choked when all the oxygen got burned in the fires. One of them propped up on an elbow and fired up at us. I remember the girl poised on the ladder below me calmly aiming her pistol to finish them off. I didn't shoot myself, I was frightened of damaging the grid with my heavier weapon. The girl had soon finished.

I glanced up the long perspective of the ladder to the light disc of sky there. Smoke straggled, framed across it I saw three hoverers, high and descending.

The girl was down on the grid and loosening bricks from the wall. When she had them out I helped her to gently unload the explosives there until she found the detonators. She cut the wires and threw the detonators into the shaft where they could do no harm. One exploded when it hit the treadmill grid and made me jump.

We went up the corridor. She knew where the charges were, she swiftly dismantled them all. Those low arches, the defensive places she took care of with radiation grenades. We killed a lot of Mods that way.

When we hit the hall where the fire used to be there were some Mods there and we had a fight on our hands. I put a bullet through Craghead's old throne and the thing dissolved in a shower of filthy dust and burning wood. It was the best thing of the day.

Maybe the guys that were shooting at us were Originals because they were pretty good. It was dark in there and they had infra-red or something so it wasn't worth the candle for us to go on. We'd secured the shaft anyway, so we went back and guarded it. We didn't have long to wait.

Three Wardens – the Superwardens – like the ones I'd thought were Aliens all that time ago up on the Tundra came floating down the shaft. For a second there it was like being back in that ruined house when that hoverer came looking for me.

"Put it down," said the girl. I had my gun coming up without knowing it. She pushed it down. "They're our men ... Free Men, if you like ... like *us!* Exploration Corps."

"But ... I ... I've killed them! Shot them down for Aliens ... I thought they were Aliens ..."

"That's over now. Relax, Ice Lover, they're friends."

"But they hunted me. Tried to catch me. You ... you saved me even when I'd burned that hoverer ... killed those men?" I remember every word I said, but it didn't make sense. I don't know what I expected.

"Of course they wanted you – there were only thirty of us on that first probe, there aren't *that* many men in all the galaxy – let alone this planet. Naturally we were interested in you ... you and that gun of yours. A special gun that can knock out a Corps battle suit. You were something special. It's my job to find out about things like that – get to know about conditions here before the main transports can come. We didn't like to lose those men – but that's the game ... they knew the risks. ... Anyway, you were the only man we found alive ... the last survivor – except that pumpman – it was my duty to save you!"

All the time she'd been talking more and more guys had been floating down the shaft. The girl told them the shaft was safe and they went on to make sure of it. They didn't take any chances. Any Mods still alive they shot, there was no mercy. They flushed the remaining Mods in front of them and the battle really got started when they met up with the Originals in the caves.

Once when we were alone for a few minutes I asked the girl why there was all the fighting. Why we couldn't just settle down with the Mods and Originals and re-build things the way they ought to be. Now the new ship had come, with all that power and equipment all sorts of things should be possible.

"They wouldn't settle," said the girl. "It's a matter of discipline. It's our world – now – we've conquered it ... conquered it twice. ... We've got to show them who are the masters. We've got to break the Originals this time ... it was a mistake to cooperate. Now we've killed the Pink we can do it. They're not human you know!"

"All right, it's them or us. But what about the Mods ... how can they be – what does it matter if they live – don't we owe them something? Why did you kill those Riders? Young Craghead's men when we went to the ship? Spite was it?" The girl was laughing at me and I didn't like that.

"Policy. We always break up formations of more than half a dozen when they're on the move. You know that."

The battle in the caves really got going about then. Those Originals weren't any pushover. They fought really hard for their own place. We won that first battle though, pretty soon the fighting degenerated into a bloody hunt through the limestone galleries. The Corps men had good sport floating and moving through the falling water and drifting smoke. The war wasn't over though, one way and another it dragged on for years – it may still be on down there for all I know. The Originals knew the caves too well – they were too big – for it to be easy. There were a lot of places the Corps men couldn't get in their battle suits and that meant the Originals always had plenty of time to get away. It was a shambles down there – a miasma of nerve gas and radiation grenades . . . all in the dark, a sort of hell.

Right then the fight was in that one big cave down there. The girl and I began to climb slowly away from it. Away from the screams and the smell of shooting. There was still steam from Rutherford's engines. They'd stopped working when the Mods there got shot. They were clicking as they cooled.

Then, on the grid nearest the surface, we found Rutherford. He was sitting there in the shadows tugging at his beard. His hair was ruffled and his eyes were wild and looked as if he'd been crying.

"My engines," was all he'd say. Shock, I guess. It must have been hell to have been in the shaft during the attack. We must have passed him on our way down, passed him for dead.

"Come up," I said. "Come and help on the surface. We can use all the Free Men there are." The girl ignored him – she never knew him like I did.

"My engines," said Rutherford again. "My books – they'll not burn my books!" He got up and walked quickly down the corridor. I called after him, but he kept on going.

"Leave him!" said the girl. "He's old – he's finished . . . he's no good to us." When I hesitated she got angry and said I'd have to choose between Rutherford and the future with her. I saw it wouldn't be a good thing to go against her right then. Then she said how a few hours in the cold and dark would have him crawling out again, so I went with her. But I didn't like it, it was the last time I ever saw him.

We made it to the surface and sat on the parapet to get our breath back. It still reeked of burning up there and there were some fresh bodies ... Mods that had been caught when the hoverers came. There hadn't been any argument then either, they'd just shot everybody. That's the great thing about Free Men, about Exploration Corps, they're efficient – when they do a thing it stays done. I thought to myself how they'd soon put the world right.

The enclosure was a sight to see. All those old weapons of Craghead's were shattered and dotted about the place, all blackened there. Then there were the acres of littered corpses scattered amongst the smoking machinery. There wasn't much fire left, it'd burned everything already. I was glad I was human and not a dead Mod.

But the thing that was really impressive, what brought it all home to me, what I can still see now, was the regular pattern of landed hoverers imposed like a silver brand on those blackened meadows. Perfect they were, shining white in the falling ash and soot ... a laid-out efficiency of serried ranks on the chaos. It was a fitting image. A symbol my mind said of the might of man and his order. I wanted to stay awhile and examine the idea but the girl got impatient. I tried to explain but it was no good of course. Those symbols were always in my mind and no one else's. There sure were a lot of dead people.

It seemed to have excited the girl. She led off to one side where there were still some trees standing. We sat down and she put her arms round my neck. Then she fell back and pulled me down on her.

"Come on!" I said. "Come on, woman! What d'you think I am? We've just come up four hundred feet of ladder!" I mean ... well!

The ground heaved. The pattern of hoverers jumped and bounced on their sprung legs. There was a long rumble deep underground.

Smoke jetted from the shaft. The whole Enclosure spouted smoke at the vents. Those great doors where they'd brought up the aeroplanes jumped vertical then slammed shut. We stood up and then fell over as the ground quaked again.

The girl shoved me off and sat up. Her breasts bobbed, she pulled her tunic shut. Her eyes were awed.

"My God! The Underground. Someone's blown the Underground!"

Rutherford! It had to be Rutherford.

"He said he'd keep his books," I said.

Then we had to go and see what had happened. The shaft was OK. The men were well enough too, shaken, but there were no casualties in those battle suits. They never found Rutherford. I don't suppose he meant to get away.

One thing, he saved his books. That first level was just a dent in the ground. I guess he had what he wanted ... but I sure wish we hadn't parted the way we did. Perhaps if I'd taken him north before the Corps came he'd be alive now. He was a good old guy, almost a father to me, and I'd left him. I still feel sad about that.

CHAPTER EIGHTEEN

IT was soon pretty clear that to survive in the sort of fighting that was going on you had to be in Exploration Corps. You had to get into one of those armoured battle suits – then you'd be a whole lot safer because then only one side would be shooting at you.

Then the girl suggested just that. Said they might probably take me if my aptitudes were right, that the Corps needed all the Free Men they could get. She said she had to go to the base in the southern hemisphere and she'd take me the same time, said she'd put in a word for me.

It was OK in the hoverer. We climbed up out of Craghead's blackened, smoking enclosure into golden morning. We swung out over the beech woods into that cloudless blue sky, the sun warm through the clear hood. We went south and high in the sweet air. They weren't really beech trees according to the girl, but hybrids of some sort. They'd been altered – modified you'd have to say – to do well in this world and planted by the first colonists. What a place! Even the trees were Mods! To me they were still beech trees. I guess real ones would have looked Alien to me.

The Borderland was sprouting green. That black barren place had a light wash of green flowing on it, thickest in the valleys. You could see places that the Corps men had begun to cultivate, getting the place ready for the new colonists. They could turn their hands to anything, those Corps men.

We crossed the Happy Land – what was left of it – and a great bare washed-out place where the crystal Mountains had been. I thought I saw the scattered buildings that had been Cristan's village, but we were high and going fast. You could see Corps men down there too – or rather their enormous machines, they could have been automatic, I suppose.

South beyond where the Mountains had been there was another such Happy Land and then another Border. It was all pretty symmetrical, there was a rightness about it, it couldn't be any other way. I said to the girl about how I was still sad it had to have been me that killed the Pink Alien and all it could have been. The girl laughed at me and said to forget it. She said it was nearly dead anyway – that her people had crept in there with their hoverers and poisoned it by stealth. She said all was fair in war.

Then there was ocean. White-surfed rocks showed dark on the sandy bottom. Then it all gave way to deep water. The girl said most of that hemisphere was water.

We flew on for maybe half an hour and then we hit a chain of islands.

Beautiful they were, all long surf and white sand beaches, palm trees, idyllic green islands on azure sea. We began losing height and circled behind a mountain with a lake in its top on the first island. That was a dead volcano according to the girl – the reason the islands were there in the first place.

We swung round the shadowed south of the volcano, over fern jungles there, we came back into sunshine and landed on a wide concrete apron there. A machine came and wheeled the hoverer away.

We stood on the concrete and I looked about me in the heat-wavering air. It was wonderful. There were low white buildings and trimmed grass, complex structures and shining tankage with spaceships in the distance. The heat kept breaking them with small mirages, they must have been five hundred feet tall and thick in proportion, like darts standing on their tails. They looked pretty big to me but they were only ferries to the starship.

A couple of men came to welcome us. They didn't have battle suits, they looked just like you or me, except they wore light breathing gear, filters across their faces. It took about a year to acclimatize to the impurities and bugs in our air, they said. I never noticed them myself, but I'm not used to sterile air in starships.

You could see the ship sometimes. It hovered stationary, not far from directly above us. It had a synchronous orbit, the girl said, it always stayed over the same place. You couldn't see it from the north – I don't suppose you were meant to.

It looked like a double moon. It was spherical – or rather it was two spheres, one of which was elongated, the shadow sides blue against the sky. You could only see the lit part, it was enormous. They told me there were only three men on board ... that was fantastic – only three men in all that vastness, it was a world to itself.

They gave me a room with a bathhouse and told me to get cleaned up for some interviews that afternoon.

The girl told me how the ship had only been there a couple of months. How all the time we were facing the Alien Pink they'd been bringing down their equipment and building their base on the island. The girl had been there long since, years, probing to find out how the first colonists from three hundred years before had survived.

The interviews were an experience too. I hardly understood a word of it. First there was this guy who wanted to play games with coloured blocks of different shapes. You had to fit them into racks and things like that. He had a sort of smoke box you had to look in, then tell him what the shapes of smoke looked like to you. He kept asking about my mother and caves, whether I felt safe or frightened in darkness, if I liked enclosed spaces, if I liked girls.

Well, if they liked playing games it was all right with me. I never ate better than when I was there, I didn't care how long I stayed. It was so quiet there, I felt *safe*, it was the way things should be.

Then they took me to see a man they called "the Doctor." He sounded my chest and poked me with silver instruments and automatic probes. He looked at my teeth too, it was like being a horse. Then he nicked my ear and they took a drop of blood away and tested that. I had to pee in a bottle for them too. The Doctor guy was very interested in my feet and the scars on my belly where I caught some shotgun pellets once.

It was all right, it seemed I was OK because I got through to the next interview and that was just talk.

There were three of them. An old guy they called "Admiral", a younger man and the girl. They were pretty splendid in their uniforms. Pale grey mostly, with a gold sunburst on the chest, they had that white and red star symbol on their arms. They were clean and cool – distinguished. Real humans.

They hadn't let me dress after the medical, so I had to stand in front of the desk with those three behind it, clutching a towel across my middle. It wasn't very dignified. I had a long wait while they went through papers. They'd taken my pistol, of course, I never felt smaller.

"So why do you want to join the Corps?" asked the young guy suddenly. "You'd have to take the field training. You'll have to give up a lot of freedom. It won't be comfortable."

"Well ... sir ... Exploration Corps – it's for men isn't it? Mankind. I'm a Free Man – human – I want to be where I belong."

"Yes, but what does the Corps mean to you?"

"It's bringing law. It'll stop the chaos and the killing, making civilization again. People will be able to settle and live happy and in peace..."

"Why should the Corps need you?"

"I know Mods. I've been in the caves. I know the Originals and I know their language." I could help, I *knew* it. When the time came to negotiate and settle I'd be valuable. "I want to be *part*, sir. I want to be a *member!*"

"Yes – and those scars, they're buckshot?" broke in the girl. "Nothing else?"

"That's what they are," said the young guy. "Nothing else!" He was laughing.

If only I could get in I knew I could help. When the Mods that were fighting – the foolish ones – were beaten, then, *then* I could help. I had enough understanding of both sides to mediate. To really help with regeneration on this world. I mean, I knew them. I wanted desperately

180

to be in the Corps anyway – a real man acknowledged by humanity.

"It's all right to laugh," said the girl, "but it could be important to me." She turned to the Admiral. "He's a good fighter."

"Yeah," said the young man. "He certainly took care of Cohen and Riley!" They must have been those two guys up on the Tundra. I'd been wondering when they'd get to that.

"You can't blame him for that," said the girl. "How was he to know? Anyway, they were careless, they asked for it."

"Yes," said the Admiral, speaking for the first time. "If a man isn't up to a job he gets killed. We only need the best in the Corps." It sounded tough to me, but I was glad he felt like that about Cohen and Riley.

The girl came round the desk and started pleading my case. She made me bend my arm to show the muscle. Then she had me turn round to show my back.

"Look," she said. "He's a good specimen. We can use men like this!" She ran her hands on my shoulders, it was like she couldn't stop touching me. "He's strong and not so stupid. Give him some training and see. He's about the last of the first colonists too – we ought to keep him, owe it to their memory – think of the propaganda!"

"All right," said the Admiral. "You want him so we'll keep him. Just keep him from shooting anyone in the meantime is all I ask." That young guy was grinning again. He sure found a lot of things funny.

They swore me in over a bible – whatever that was – and said I should start the training right away.

They had dandy ways of training you. That Field Trainer thing was an "encephalic dome" which fitted right down over your head, took all your senses away and gave you new ones with more besides. I don't remember too much about it because I was drugged and that was all part of the process as well. I know they brought me out every so often and there were all sorts of tests and simulators. Every time they did that it seemed I knew a bit more – like how to read and write properly or I suddenly found I could strip the ring locks on an ion unit. Mostly it was like being crazy with fever, I only remember it as a long period of hallucinations – which is a word I didn't know before.

The last time they woke me they seemed very pleased, said I was a good subject. They brought me fully back to consciousness and told me I was cleared for promotion all the way up to commissioned rank, but I'd have to take a "Consolidating Training" within the next year otherwise it might all slip away again. I sure knew a lot of things though, they just kept welling up in my mind as I needed them – I thought the Corps were wonderful before, but now I knew they were gods ... that training was great.

I was tired though. It was like I'd been ill, or working really hard for weeks. I felt feeble and full of age. Then they told me the whole thing had taken about four hours, that it was the same day and I was a trained Corps man! It was like magic, but I sure was tired. They gave me a drink and I started to think I might live.

That night the girl came and we made love. It was the only time I ever had her, or she me, I suppose. She was my only Free Woman too – it wasn't like a Breeder. She seemed to have it in her head that I was going into some terrible danger and she'd never see me again. It seemed as if she was exaggerating to me – but she kept on and on about it, she was so sure the Originals were going to get me and the idea seemed to excite her. Maybe that was why she kept working at it. I wasn't so sure I liked her so much after all.

The next morning they sent me north and I joined the fighting.

It wasn't so different. Corps men had to be just as tough and fast as any Free Man up on the Tundra. I thought the weapons we used were a bit heavy – those burners attached to our chests for example – but with a battle suit it doesn't matter too much. Anyway we had pistols like my old one too. All those flashing gauge lights on your front take a bit of following, training or no training. There's a lot to watch if you're a Corps man.

182

We sure chopped down those Mods. At first there was only what was left of Craghead's men to hunt through the woods but then the Corps started an extermination policy and when the Mods caught onto that they all started fighting. They were in league with the Originals too – unless the Corps gets those caves flushed out there'll never be peace.

I fought everywhere – all the campaigns – except in the caves. That was a specialist job by the time I was involved. There were some Corps men got really good down there, enjoyed it they did – trained to it, I suppose. But like I said before it's so big down there the war could go on forever.

About then the Corps gave up the first island base and moved up to where Craghead's Enclosure used to be. I guess it was to get to be near the caves, that entrance was still the only big one we were sure of. We'd lost a hundred men in the caves already – that's 10 per cent of the total available manpower – it was very costly down there in that hell of radiations and fire. In one place they'd tried to get the Originals by burning all the air down there, the fires we lit will burn a hundred years ... make vast dangerous areas of quicklime too ... it's horrible down there when it rains. Anyway, the point was we were losing too many men on the way to the regeneration bays on the ship. Some of the guys that died could have been resurrected if the trip to the bays had been quicker, so they brought the ship down real low above the Enclosure.

The ship used to rise and set three or four times a day. Sometimes, when it got too low, you could see the undersides glowing and burning as it brushed the atmosphere. When that happened they turned on the power and it lifted again.

I saw the girl sometimes. She looked really good in her officer's suit. She saw me too, but never spoke – like I say, she was an officer. Anyway, I guess she'd had what she wanted.

They had a kind of museum there too. Just inside where those gates used to be. I suppose it was to impress any tame Mods there might be and to encourage us. There was old machinery there, poor Old Rutherford's pathetic engines for one thing, stuff from the first colonization too. All mounted it was – on marble blocks they found some place.

They had Craghead there too – stuffed. It didn't make him look any better. There was one of those multi-carapaces there too. They'd killed the Originals in it with radiation grenades so it was spoiled with burns. They had models of the Think modified in it, so you could see what it had been like. There were plenty of Thinkers by the way, you know the way Mods breed.

I kept getting depressed again. There was something mad about it – fanatical. Like it was religious. The officers kept saying it was our world – ours alone. Sure it was, we'd taken it, so it was ours . . . but not in the way they meant it. They were so insistent – kept on and on about it – telling us, I couldn't see why. I mean, we knew already. Then they gave that extermination order. It was mad. We should have concentrated on the Originals in their caves – they were plenty to take on – instead of stirring the Mods up again.

It seemed to me we should make a deal. It would have been the *right* thing to settle with the Mods. They were beaten, there was no need to wipe them out. We could make peace, we could live together. But you got court-martialled for talk like that, so I didn't say anything.

Actually what was happening to me was the training hadn't taken – I had a lot of my own mind left and the rest was coming out of it. That accounted for the depression too, the way everything seemed mad. It was only a Field Training they gave me.

The last straw came when our platoon was out on a sweep through the beech woods. Right on top of the base we were – fighting Mods on our own doorstep. After five years! We didn't have our hoverers, not that close to base. We were after a group of Breeders that had been reported going north.

It was evening, I was sitting in the roots of a dead tree – all the trees were dead in that part – listening to some

184

radiation bombing up north. There was some wood-smoke drifting across the clearing and you could smell some Mod bodies we were burning. There was a hoverer burning quietly about a mile away and you could hear a Mod who had a sort of anthrax he'd been sprayed with screaming while a couple of our guys tried to make him talk. The moon was up and that was beautiful.

Then a hoverer dropped over the trees and who should get out but the girl. She had a new man, a replacement, with her and she brought him over towards me.

"Your new sergeant," she said. "I've brought him up." It was young Craghead.

Sure, I knew they were short of men and they were recruiting some of the less grotesque Mods – training them and putting them against their own kind. But young Craghead! Seeing him there was a surprise – I thought he was dead for one thing.

Thinking about it though, I could see that if any Mod was going to be a renegade it'd be him. He would brain-wash pretty easy – you could convince him water ran uphill . . . if you thought it was worth it.

"He's the first," said the girl. "The first Mod to complete his training. We've made him sergeant to encourage others." It was the last straw. I was still a corporal.

I decided then, in that moment. There were other reasons too – all the cruelty, all the needless slaughter, the extermination policy, the weapons we were using.

I deserted. I spun on my heel. It was all wrong. I'd killed enough. I fought for the Corps and this was the end of it. I wasn't human enough to kill any more Mods.

I walked quickly between the girl and Craghead. Their smiles faded. I walked past the beaten prisoners, past the burning piles of bodies. I made it almost to the hoverer before the girl called out after me.

The gold I had towards buying my commission was heavy in my pocket. You've got to keep gold close to you in the Corps or people steal it. I dumped it out and turned on my battle suit.

"Keep your damn Corps!" I yelled. "I'm not your sort – I'm on the wrong goddamn side!" I was crying.

185

Then the girl started to shoot at me with that little pistol of hers. She blew a hole in the hoverer's canopy and then hit me in the chest. She was smiling.

Battle suits are pretty good so I only got knocked down. By reflex I had my pistol out and fired back. I missed her but my shots sucked her off her feet and dumped her really hard into the trees. She didn't move again, I guess it broke every bone in her body, she didn't have a battle suit, and that was her hard luck.

Craghead cut in his suit and soared into the air. Like a great angel he was up there ... or a black fly buzzing against the sky while we tried to draw a bead on each other. I hit him twice and the third shot got his fuel cell. He crashed down in flames and burned like that guy in the Tundra.

I tumbled into the hoverer and grabbed the up lever. At fifty feet I cut loose with all the ordnance. It was dangerous so low – you can get caught in your own explosions – but it sure burned down there and so did the Corps men who were shooting at me. If the girl had been still alive she was dead then and I suppose I didn't care.

Don't think I like killing people, some of those Corps men were friends – well, as near as you can get to be friends with people – but it was them or me. I suppose that's what they all say.

So I made it north. As fast as that stolen hoverer would carry me. I brought it down in a gully at the far north edge of the pinewoods. Then I punched a hole in the tank and started a fire in the pine needles where it would reach the fuel.

I threw the armoured part of my suit in the cabin and went on north in the rest of it, the survival kit. It was cold where I was going and it'd be a while before I could get any furs. You can bet I kept my pistol and ammunition too.

That hoverer burned for a whole day. I could see the smoke plume behind me and the other hoverers buzzing about like flies there. For a long time then I was by myself and that was good.

CHAPTER NINETEEN

So I've come full circle back to the Tundra. Out in the cold again, ready to disappear into the convoluted ice-maze glaciers when, sometimes, the hoverers come. They hunted me from time to time, but they'll never find anything they're looking for in the ice, perhaps they've forgotten me. But really I know they'll kill me one day ... they'll kill everybody else too, so what does it matter?

There's four Mods and me now. I've armed them from that cache of weapons in the range that Rutherford found. I'll arm any Mod that comes and asks. They've accepted me, they know what I've done, deeds are stronger than words – they're stronger than race too, I've found that out.

That Mod that used to sing at Craghead's – he showed up the other day. He still sings but he lost his instrument so it isn't so good. He sings about going to the wall, about melting and dying, lost purpose and opportunity. They stand Mods against a wall to shoot them – that's where it comes from – it's a tradition. We do the same to Corps men, when we catch them. I'm not going to any wall.

There's a spot or two of hope. I've heard there are some other Corps men who've joined the fight on our side. They've had too much of it as well. There are Mods fighting for the Corps too, it's not one-sided. Maybe it's a sign we can join together one day – there's hope there, I tell myself. I know we could if we let ourselves.

I think I'm on the right side. Sometimes, in spite of the cold – to reassure myself, I take off my leggings and my boots and look at my feet.

I've got twelve toes you see – and they're webbed. So maybe I'm a Mod. They're anthrax bombing in the south again and I hope I'm a Mod.

They – the Mods, us – we're the true inheritors. The

two races are so alike – men and Originals – and we Mods, we're the outcome. A combination – love between us all is the only answer. The Mods can show it's possible. Think of it! Peace and fulfilment for everybody. It could be paradise.

When I joined the Corps, at the medical, when they were so interested in my feet, they said then that human babies are born like that sometimes. They said the doctors tie off the extra toes with thread and they wither off ... the children then grow up normal – with ten toes. The Corps Doctor didn't seem to think it was important.

It sounded like a fairy tale to me. Something they made up to keep me happy, to get me to join the Corps. I was glad enough to believe it at the time. I hope it was a fairy tale, I hope I'm on the right side. I keep counting my toes and hoping.

Anyway, I know what I'm going to do. There's something I can do to make it better. It's a fate for me, a destiny ... a *big* thing. It's symbolic too, I can see that.

Ever since that first day up on the Tundra I've been falling into things ... going into caves. Craghead's Underground for example, or the crystal Mountains, the Originals' caves or that Charcoal Burner's hut, even that underpass I fell in when I dived from that house at the very beginning. That guy with the coloured blocks and the smoke box that kept asking me about dark places and girls, he was interested in it too. Fool. I could tell him – it's my destiny. He asked about dying too – I could tell him that too ... I don't mind. That's destiny as well.

I know a way into the Underground. There were lots of exits, the girl knew that ... if she's dead she won't have told the Corps. You can still find a tortuous way through those collapsed tunnels. I know ... I've been ... on a reconnaissance once.

Those thermonuclear warheads, they're still there. They were made to be good forever, they've been prayed for, they'll still be good.

I'll take a candle and a springy branch – hazel maybe. I'll fix radiation grenades in the warheads and tie the caps to the bent stick. I'll hold it bent with cord and stand the candle against it. I'll light the candle and when it burns the cord the stick will straighten like a bow and pull the caps off the grenades. I've got it all worked out.

When the grenades explode that terrible burst of radiation'll touch off those warheads, right under the Corps main base. They won't know even what's happened.

If I'm lucky it may get the ship as well. Anyway, if it doesn't, what can three men do? They'll just go home. There'll be a lot of damage ... radiation for a few years. We'll live through that — what difference do a few mutations make to a race like we Mods? By the time they get back with reinforcements we'll be ready for them ... if they think it's worth coming a third time that is.

It's a thick candle ... a black one ... it'll burn five hours. I'll have a stripped-down hoverer waiting for me when I get out .. it shouldn't take more than three hours to make it out, I should be able to get clear of the explosion. If I don't, so what?

After the bang, with their base and leaders gone, maybe the Corps survivors will stop fighting and make peace. Maybe we can join together and get to something important like making the world right again. The same goes for the Originals. Maybe it'll just take those warheads to bring them to their senses ... a short sharp lesson for everybody. That second ship of Colonists that's on the way — one of the renegade Corps men told me it's mostly full of women. They won't be like Breeders, but if they land they'll be welcome.

I'm going tomorrow. We can't get any further north anyway, we've got to do something. I hope to get into the pine trees by dawn. A week after that I should be in the Underground. I'll sure light a last candle for someone and something then.

I've been sitting here waiting for the moon to rise. That singing guy has been singing some corny old earth song about the moon and June, about love and lovers. It's pretty poor really ... sad too, sadder the more you think of it.

One thing though. In my training — in the astronomi-

189

cal knowledge they gave me – it was quite clear that this planet is unique in the galaxy in having one moon ... among habitable worlds that is. From the song the earth's only got one too. You'd think the Corps would have a thing like that right, wouldn't you? Maybe it's poetic licence.

So long as it's not my world I don't mind touching off those warheads ... like I say ... I don't *enjoy* killing people, but what can you do?

Science Fiction in Tandem editions

Name ....

Address..

Titles required ....

....

....

....

....

....

....

- -

The publishers hope that you enjoyed this book and invite you to write for the full list of Tandem titles which is available free of charge.

If you find any difficulty in obtaining these books from your usual retailer we shall be pleased to supply the titles of your choice — packing and postage 5p — upon receipt of your remittance.

WRITE NOW TO:
      Universal-Tandem Publishing Co. Ltd.,
      14 Gloucester Road,
      London SW7